Forever Falls

Michael Warren Lucas

For Liz

By the Same Author

Immortal Clay
Kipuka Blues
Butterfly Stomp Waltz
Hydrogen Sleets
git commit murder

Nonfiction (as Michael W Lucas):

Relayd and Httpd Mastery – PAM Mastery – FreeBSD Mastery: Advanced ZFS
– FreeBSD Mastery: Specialty Filesystems – FreeBSD Mastery: ZFS –
Tarsnap Mastery – Networking for Systems Administrators –
FreeBSD Mastery: Storage Essentials – Sudo Mastery – DNSSEC Mastery –
Absolute OpenBSD – SSH Mastery – Network Flow Analysis –
Absolute FreeBSD – Cisco Routers for the Desperate – PGP & GPG

See your favorite bookstore for more!

1

Most universes don't get an official name, only a number, but for obvious reasons everyone called this place Freefall.

This universe also had the messiest corpse I'd ever seen.

Devin Gupper, experimental mathematician and metallurgist, looked like he'd lost an argument with an orbital mass driver. His remnants lay crushed against the steel surface of the Debris Shield. Broken bones jabbed through his torn flesh. Blood dries normally in Freefall, but his uniform was still drenched.

I breathed through my mouth and demanded my stomach still itself. *You will not throw up. You are Aidan Redding, security third and the toughest damn woman in this universe. You volunteered to come out here, and you will* not *throw up.* I insisted that I believed myself, but I felt pretty sure I was lying on all counts.

Security Second Ella Forecourt knelt beside the body, her thin face thoughtful as she studied the wreck of Gupper's body. "I can't say for sure—we need to get him down to Medical and get a proper autopsy." Ella had to raise her voice above her normal papery rasp to be heard above the constant rustle of wind. "But this doesn't look like a beating." The dinner-platter helmet perched on her head made her gaunt frame look even thinner.

"What then?" I really didn't want to take another breath. There's something extra horrible about the smell of a totally broken body, how everything that belongs inside you gets mixed into this gut-stabbing stench. I'd seen bodies before—you couldn't spend your first year out of college working security for the Montague Corporation, exploring and exploiting alien universes with different natural laws, without someone having a heart attack or getting assaulted by antimatter-propelled chipmunks or discovering that the grass would eat your face on alternate Tuesdays.

But Devin Gupper's death was the most spectacular and messy yet.

Forecourt looked up at me. "I'd say he fell."

I couldn't help it. I looked up.

The Debris Shield is a steel awning, about ten meters across and a hundred long, mounted in a long notch hacked in the jagged green-and-gray granite cliff. It reflected the endless sunlight with a brilliant silver shine you could probably see for kilometers. So long as I confined my gaze to the riveted and dent-pocked surface beneath my magnetic boots, I could pretend the steel deck was in a normal facility.

Looking up shattered that illusion.

The cliff goes up forever. No, it doesn't *look* like it goes on forever. It really does. A stone horizon splits the sky and circles around left and right. The sky glares the red of a volcanic sunset.

The whole universe hung sideways. The only solid surface was this vertical cliff, with the Montague facility clinging to its face like a desperate ant.

Fall off the edge and you'll never hit bottom.

Humans couldn't live here. Life couldn't even evolve here. The Portal's mathematical transformations changed us so we could survive, but the only living things in this whole universe were the ones we had brought with us.

Montague engineers hadn't built anything above the Debris Shield. That was the point of the Shield, to protect the facility from intermittent falling pebbles. If a rock came free directly over us, a hundred feet up or a hundred kilometers, it would eventually ping off the Debris Shield instead of my skull. Or anyone else's. The sloping surface encouraged everything to bounce away from the facility below.

I never feared heights on Earth. But this looming, lifeless infinity gnawed at my soul. My magnetic boots and hemp safety line seemed inadequate against forever.

Gupper had disappeared seventeen hours ago. And he reappeared, just now, atop the Debris Shield. Had he climbed the cliff? What for?

"Redding!"

I jerked my attention back. After two months of inspecting cargo and airing the uniform, volunteering to climb onto the Debris Shield had sounded good. Apparently I wasn't up for it yet.

Forecourt looked at me, head cocked. "The sooner you take the pix, the sooner we can get under cover."

Freefall didn't faze Forecourt at all. *Okay, Redding you're second toughest woman here. Still, get your act together!*

I fumbled for the optical camera dangling from my neck. We both wore broad helmets and heavy padded impact suits, but a pebble at terminal velocity would still leave a mark.

Back on Earth, sousveillance cameras would have caught Gupper's impact in life-definition video. If I'd needed actual photos, I would have used optic implants to suck in everything and sort out the good shots later. Digital cameras didn't work on Freefall, let alone implants, and this camera only had thirty sheets of light-sensitive paper. I needed to capture Gupper from every angle in thirty shots, without touching his body and without letting my shadow cross the image, all with equipment three centuries obsolete.

Freefall doesn't have a sun. It has many, a column of giant fuzzy orbs of fuming amber majestically plunging from the top of infinity to the very bottom, out in the middle of the hazy red sky. The red sky behind me, and below. So long as I didn't stand where Gupper and I made a perpendicular line from the cliff, the yellow-red orbs shed enough light for the optical paper to work.

Peering through the tiny glass viewfinder, I framed Gupper's black hair and a shoulder. The camera felt clunky in my gloved hands. At a press of the lever, the camera whirred to release a piece of plastic-coated paper no wider than my hand.

I set the exposed paper on the deck to dry, mindful not to touch the surface where the photograph would appear, and moved on to the next angle.

My magnetic boots clanked at each step. I got halfway around Gupper and had to circle back around to avoid dragging the safety line through the pool of coppery blood drying on the deck.

I'd joined Montague to see the universes, all the universes, not move shattered bodies.

Frame fractured flesh. Click. Whirr.

Thirty pictures isn't enough to really document a death scene, but I split them as best I could. Despite the breeze, when I finished sweat covered my face. My stomach had seethed itself into a turgid knot, but I kept my gorge down even with intermittent surges of bile at the back of my throat.

"Good," Forecourt said as I clicked the last photo, studying the images coalescing on the exposed films. "I can see why Montague put you on camera duty, you have a real eye for this. Now help me get him in the bag and down to Medical, and we'll see if we can figure out how he died."

I'm proud to say all three of us made it off the Debris Shield and behind safety rails before my lunch broke free.

2

Doctor Cleese took one look at Gupper's shattered remains and declared that he'd fallen. He took a few test samples, stuffed my death scene photos into Gupper's medical file, and sent Forecourt and I on our way. I hadn't gotten any blood on myself, but after stripping out of the impact armor I grabbed a quick shower in the locker room just to steam the stench from my sinuses. I came back to my locker, where I'd left my Montague uniform folded on a bench, and found a slip of paper on my khakis. *Find out why Gupper went up there – Forecourt.*

Forecourt supervised Facility security. I guess she had something more important to do than investigate the first accidental death on Freefall since the construction crew dug us into the cliff. I'd met every one of the one hundred and nine— eight people at the Freefall base, and vaguely remembered Gupper as the one of the maniacs who worked in the Diffusion lab, dangling from a zeppelin out in the haze. But a few of the Diffusion folks worked here.

And at least the Diffusion folks were less obsessed than the neutronium miners.

I slipped into my khakis, fastened the brass buckles on my boots, checked that my radio and taser were firmly clipped to my belt, and set out.

Where Medical and Security were buried inside the granite, the Diffusion lab clung to the outside of the cliff, supported steel girders driven a yard deep into the stone and high-tension cables strung up to the next layer of girders. At orientation they told me that the whole facility looked like an old North American pre-conquest cliff-dweller city. Better still, three of the Diffusion lab's walls were clear glass—no, not plasteel, but actual, old-fashioned, so-called "shatterproof" glass. I'd been through here on my orientation tour and never felt the need to return.

The lab was normally quietly busy, the only sounds the occasional power tool or mathematical discussion. Now four people stood in a tight knot amidst lab tables and sample bins and dangling spotlights and tools. Stacked notebooks and binders filled the spaces where computers would sit in a lab on Earth, and shelves of thick paper books lined the inner wall. Computers didn't work on Freefall.

Voices hoarse with grief cut off when I swung the door open. News traveled faster than I did.

Haider Takamoto, mathematician and director of the Diffusion Lab, turned to face me and visibly steeled his round features. "Da?"

"Hello," I said. "I'm Aidan Redding, from Security. I know this is a hard time, but I need to ask you some questions about Devin Gupper."

"What was he doing up there?" a tiny woman said. Her name danced on the tip of my tongue, but the text over her shirt pocket reminded me.

"Miss Pouter, I was hoping you could help me find out," I said. "He worked with you fairly often."

"About half the time," Takamoto said. "Always the hope to stay here more, but his experiments drag him out to the Hindenbarge, da?"

That Ukraine Union accent can't *be real. Can it?* "What exactly were his duties, Doctor Takamoto?"

Takamoto turned to the other woman in the room.

I knew Doctor Cedar. You couldn't help noticing her. Redheads had become increasingly rare over the centuries, but some fluke of genetic chance had given Cedar copper-bright hair and a frame a handspan too tall for any other woman. A thousand years past, she would have manned the pikes just like the Irishmen around her and dared anyone to argue.

People called her Paddy. But not to her face.

"We were working on titanium," Cedar said, her voice tight. "Building models, floating them out into the diffusion zone, seeing if we could make a strong, stable, diffuse titanium."

"Don't we mostly diffuse steel?" I asked.

She nodded. Tears glistened in her green—*green*—eyes, but the set of her jaw would have cracked anyone else's bones. "Diffuse steel is profitable, but diffuse titanium would have been twenty-eight times so."

"You could have done it," said the fourth person, perched on his padded stool.

Cedar turned to glare at him, anger seeping through every word. "You told him it was stupid at every turn, Marcus."

Marcus shrugged his bony shoulders. "Male bonding." He ran his fingers through his curly Mediterranean hair. "You know. Just.. bullshit." His voice grew soft. "But he knew his stuff, or he wouldna been here. You two woulda whupped it. I had a hundred on next month in the pool."

The Montague Corporation's ridiculous return on investment meant they paid the best salaries in the world, and they were choosy on who they took on board. I had no doubt of Gupper's professional abilities.

Just his climbing ones.

Cedar shuddered, fighting back passions roused by Marcus' ambush of support.

Takamoto reached her side half a heartbeat later. "Is okay to cry." He put a solicitous hand on her shoulder. "Devin deserves a tear."

Cedar's chest shook for a moment, then she turned away from us, letting Takamoto's hand fall.

Takamoto's face flickered through worry, irritation, and distress. His eyes followed Cedar.

I knew the look. He had hopes, hopes involving Cedar and himself. With her unique look Cedar had probably caught the eyes of every man in Freefall, and kept half of them.

"I know it's hard," I said, "but I have to ask. Do any of you know why Gupper went above the debris shield?"

"He wouldn't have," Marcus said. "Not a chance in hell."

"Why?" I said.

"He hated it here," Pouter said, his hands idly twisting a circular slide rule. "Said he wanted solid ground underfoot."

I wished she hadn't said that. For a second I felt the emptiness beneath me. Yes, the facility had half a dozen more levels beneath me. The complex had roots sunk deep into the granite behind me. But for the space of a breath, the endless plummet sucked at my feet.

"We have our own floaters," Pouter continued. "If he ever wanted to go above the shield, he'd check one out and fly up."

"Was he—" Marcus coughed. "Was he wearing climbing gear?"

I thought back. Blood had soaked his clothes, but they'd looked like the usual Montague-issued khakis and loose-fitting shirt. His shoes had been the slip-on gum-soled corporate issue as well. You had to work security or construction to get boots. And the construction guys didn't get the bronze buckles. "No."

Cedar turned to face me. "If Devin got it in his fool head to climb above the shield, he'd have worn armor. He'd have the boots, the ropes, the gloves, the grappling hook gun. Devin liked the toys."

I frowned. "When did you see him last?"

Takamoto said "Yesterday. End of day." A sun, huge and fuzzy, loomed outside, its red light pouring through the tinted window. It had inched down in the few minutes I stood there. Even if that sun set, another hung right above it to take its place. Like so many other universes, our clock was a mutually agreeable fiction.

I peered around the room, trying to look past the work surfaces and drafting tables and hanging metal-working gear. "You said you had floaters?"

"He would not have," Takamoto said. "No."

"Devin didn't even like the zeppelin," Cedar said. "If he wanted something from above the shield, he would have had someone else float up and get it."

"And he had—" I glanced at my watch. "Eighteen hours to find someone to do that."

Cedar's face twisted.

I resisted the urge to pounce. "Excuse me, Doctor?"

Cedar looked like she tasted something bad.

Pouter peered up at Cedar. "Well, out with it!" She flung her hands in the air. "It's not like we don't all know."

Takamoto's eyes grew as round as his face.

"Know what?" said Marcus.

Pouter glanced between the two men. "All right then. The smart ones knew." She snorted. "Everyone with an innie."

"I saw Devin this morning," Cedar said. "Before breakfast."

I carefully didn't notice Cedar's rising blush. Researchers get touchy about those things. "So, about ten hours ago then."

"He said he needed to check some samples here." Cedar's voice sounded quieter than ever. "We were going out to the Hindenbarge today. Devin said he'd meet me in the mess hall."

"Did he?" I asked.

Cedar shook her head.

"You should have said," Takamoto said, forcing a smile over his stormy expression.

"It's not your business," Cedar said. "It's not anybody's business."

It's my business, I didn't say. I can be tactful.

"I did payroll at my desk this morning," Takamoto said. "Was due at noon. Paperwork, always paperwork. He never show up."

"If he had snuck in and flown up," Pouter said, "we would have seen him."

"The floaters have been here all day," Marcus said.

The floor of the Diffusion Lab felt tenuous enough. I wanted to walk back into the nice stable granite.

"I better check these floaters," I said.

3

The Diffusion Lab felt uncomfortable enough, with its glass walls suspended over the infinite void. I did not want to go outside it, into the open air.

But I'd wanted to see the universes. When the job tells you to walk through a door, you walk through it.

Doctor Takamoto led me around a freestanding cabinet to a door where the glass wall met smooth polished green-flecked granite. The glass door swung open at a touch, letting the warm sirocco flow around us as we stepped out onto the steel mesh walkway.

My eyes blinked in the sudden light. This side of the Diffusion lab stuck out further east than any other level of the Freefall facility. The warm wind rising through the walkway smelled of a dusty desert that hadn't seen rain for centuries and never expected to see it again. I instinctively grabbed the steel pipe rail separating the walkway from the long drop all around us.

I kept my eyes on Takamoto.

"Is impressive, nyet?" Takamoto said, raising a hand. "Is closest we get to Forever Falls. Without flying, of course."

You have to speak well to work for Montague. That accent has *to be deliberate. Doesn't it?*

Takamoto's arm pointed up. I had looked straight up earlier today. I intended to never do it again. But I made myself raise my head and follow his arm to look at the waterfall.

The waterfall tumbled from infinitely far overhead, coursing down the granite, splashing and spraying as it bounced between worn crannies of stone. The steaming red light sparkled off the spray, glittering gems that dissolved into the air. You couldn't help but look up, trying to trace its origin, and wind up peering into the infinite sky.

We were close enough to the waterfall to hear water surge and gush as it poured between the rocks. My hands ached to reach for the water, even though it fell meters beyond my reach. The air's parched dryness made the torrent feel like a taunt.

I'd heard the reverse physicists arguing about the waterfall over dinner more than once. The flowing water should have dissolved into spray, and then into vapor, within a few kilometers of wherever it started. The fact that it didn't meant that they didn't understand Freefall's physical laws as well as they thought they did.

Montague researchers had taken zeppelins up almost forty kilometers and down another forty, where the hazy air made the facility invisible and the electromagnetic interference made radio communication almost impossible. The waterfall ran all the way. As far as we could tell, the waterfall ran forever.

I traced the waterfall down, seeing it skip and splash from eternity to a point where it felt I should be able to touch it, and then receding again back down into forever—

—and I stared into the abyss.

It's one thing to look up and see the cliff face recede into eternity. You can look to left and right and see the cliff marching on and on. But most of us, when we look down, have that little monkey part of the brain that starts shrieking *There's no ground.*

There. Is. No. Ground.

The cliff face descends forever.

The only thing beneath the metal walkway was burnt amber sky.

For a split second, my mind tried to convince itself that I was sideways, lying on the ground. But that didn't work either. The cliff was too flat, the pull of gravity too strong.

One wrong step and I'd fall. Into the sky.

My stomach knotted again, and my hands clamped around the railing. My pulse hammered in my ears even as my breath froze solid.

Takamoto said something.

I tried to swallow, and couldn't.

The breeze flowed past me, rising. No, it wasn't rising. My gut plummeted, we were all falling—

Something seized me and shook.

I jerked.

Takamoto had his arm around my bicep. "Redding!" His Ukraine accent made my name almost unintelligible.

I met Takamoto's eyes. Sweat soaked the back of my shirt and my armpits, and tension strained my every muscle. My head quivered on my neck. The warm breeze suddenly felt cool over my face.

On my first day in Freefall, Pete from HR took me to the observation deck at the edge of the dirigible hangar and let me have a good look. This second look hadn't been any better.

"I am sorry." The accent faded. He sounded almost gentle. "You learn to ignore it. We do, at least." His lips twitched downward. A touch of bitterness leaked back into his voice when he added "Most of us."

I drew a shaky breath. "It's okay." Had Takamoto truly forgotten what most of us felt looking down the cliff? Or had his disappointment over Cedar and Gupper led him to minor cruelty?

"This way," he said, holding a hand along the walkway.

The metal balcony circled the Diffusion lab. I clutched the steel pipe rail as we turned the corner and started along the long way. The Debris Shield loomed floors above us like an awning, but offered no shade whatsoever from the horizontal suns.

"I come out here at lunch," Takamoto said. "This morning, breakfast. Sit on edge, let my feet dangle over, watch water fall. Peaceful." He chuckled. "Lost a shoe once. Supply clerk most upset. Had to insist I was *very* sure shoe not lost in quarters."

I kept my eyes on his back.

The floaters were at the far side of the balcony, on a wide launch platform. Each had a battery pack and two meter-wide fans, one pointed back, the other up. You would wear a flight suit and a self-packing parasail, letting the one fan blow you up and the other push you forward. It wouldn't work on Earth, but on Freefall, floaters were the easiest way to maneuver around the cliff. You stood on the platform, tugged the parasail trigger, and let the fans carry you away.

The Diffusion lab had two floater racks. Both floaters had a locking plastic strap with a date tag around its frame, tying it to the launch platform. Someone could take a floater any time they needed, but then a Transit flunky would replace the tag. Without computers, and with radio spotty at more than a couple kilometers, the facility relied on these kinds of tricks to keep track of equipment use.

Nobody had used the one floater for a week, the other for three days.

Takamoto glanced at me, then at the floaters, and shook his head. "However he got up there," Takamoto said, "it wasn't with our floaters."

I glanced at the window. The glass reflected my silhouette, surrounded by the glare of the falling suns. Inside that room were three people who insisted that Gupper would not have climbed above the shield.

I'd have to check the rest of the floaters, but I was beginning to think they were right.

Gupper would have only gotten up above the Debris Shield if someone had taken him there.

If I planned to meet a new lover for breakfast, I wouldn't have gone climbing or floating.

That meant someone must have taken Gupper up there.

Someone knew how he died. I could only think of one reason for them to keep silent.

Gupper hadn't fallen.

He'd been pushed.

4

Gupper had last been seen around seven AM. His body had appeared on the Debris Shield at half past four. Nine and a half hours. I spent another hour gathering and checking facts before rapping on Security Second Forecourt's door. My feet hurt and my eyes ached in their sockets. I'd been up early to start a long day, and if Forecourt granted my request it promised to be longer.

"Come in."

Forecourt's granite-walled office barely fit her, the raw granite desk, and two uncomfortably rickety office chairs. When adding a cubic inch means carving it out of granite, every space is as small as possible. Air tainted with machine oil whispered through a narrow ceiling vent. Two pole lamps in the corners shed light, which reflected off the unpolished green and gray ceiling. Every time I came here, I fought the urge to shade my eyes against the glare.

"Redding." Forecourt put her blue pencil down next to the paper on her desk. Earth ran on computers, but those of us in Montague grew accustomed to places where computers didn't work. "Report."

I stood straight and clasped my hands behind my back. "I've talked to Gupper's team, Surveillance, and Transit."

Forecourt's eyes bore into the point just between and above my eyebrows. "And?" Quiet background music would have smothered her soft voice.

"Something doesn't make sense, ma'am."

"Do tell."

"Gupper's team insists that he wouldn't have climbed up. He hated leaving the building. And he wasn't wearing climbing gear."

"But he was up there."

"I've checked with Transit. All the floaters are accounted for."

Forecourt leaned back in her chair. "So he must have climbed."

"I spoke with both daytime operators. Neither saw anything."

"The cameras don't have perfect coverage." The Montague Corporation's total border paranoia policy was somewhat relaxed in lifeless universes. "And we can't record."

"But there's cameras pointing straight down all three ladders above the Shield. And the daily reporting keeps the camera crew mostly alert."

"What about the overnight crew?" Forecourt asked.

"Gupper was seen by a member of his team before breakfast today." I shifted my feet. It had already been a long day.

She raised a thin finger to tap her lips. "Indeed. And why didn't this person say so earlier?"

"Doctor Cedar felt that the way she saw him was none of our business." I gave a thin smile.

"I see. And were you able to corroborate her story?"

"One of the canteen crew, McDevitt, reported seeing him this morn. Gupper grabbed a coffee on his way to the lab. He was whistling."

"And the canteen crew didn't report him?"

"McDevitt didn't realize who it was until I showed him a photo. Not those photos, ma'am."

Forecourt arched an eyebrow. "I assumed not *those* photos, Redding. The ones you took this morning didn't show Gupper's face except as an imprint in the back of his skull."

I fought the blush that threatened to creep up the back of my neck. I'd learned to control my attitude when I wanted something, but Forecourt could snark at her subordinates all she wanted. "Yes, ma'am."

"So," Forecourt said. "He wouldn't have climbed up, he wasn't dressed to climb, and he didn't take a floater. Do you think he hitched a ride on a zeppelin, and it detoured so he could jump out?"

"The last people who saw him reported he was happy," I said. "He wouldn't have jumped."

Forecourt snorted. "Are you saying—you are, aren't you? You think he was—" The corner of her mouth quirked. "—*pushed*?"

"Ma'am."

"Okay then." The smile came out of hiding. Forecourt leaned forward, put her elbows on her desk, and steepled her fingers. "What do you want to do about it?"

I took a deep breath. "A zeppelin arrived this morning and left an hour later. If anyone on the flight in had seen anything, the passengers would have said something. But six people, counting the pilot, flew back. And nobody's been back since."

"So you want to meet the next zeppelin and talk to any of those six who come back, then catch the flight out the next day."

"No, ma'am. I want a zeppelin to the Hindenbarge now."

The snort became a laugh. "A special?"

"Ma'am, those people might come back by ones and twos all week long. If I have to talk to them one at a time it will take days. I'll have to wait until there's a morning none of them come back, and catch the zeppelin then."

"I could send word with the next zeppelin. Tell them to come back the next morning."

My spine twitched with added tension. "The longer I wait, the longer they have to get a story together."

"And you're going to interrogate them," Forecourt said. "Oh, that's right, your degree is Criminal Justice, isn't it? Do they still do the virtual interrogation thing?"

"Virtual and role-play." *Oh, that sounds* great, *Redding. Now tell her you dressed up in a cowboy hat to play Thugs and Natives with the neighborhood kids.*

"Well, then, you have it all sorted out, don't you? Well, we have spare zeppelins, and those pilots just hang around picking their toenails. You can carry some messages for me while you go. Wear your metal-free uniform."

I felt a surge of victory, then Forecourt said "Tell me, Redding. Have you ever been to the Hindenbarge?"

"No, ma'am."

"They have their own security detail out there. And Security Second Lundbaugh is not as warm and fuzzy as I am." Forecourt's smile evaporated. "You will *not* make us look bad."

I fought back a grin. "Yes, ma'am." I'd grab my best uniform and pull out my fancy etiquette.

"That means," Forecourt said, "no puking your guts out over the rail. Again."

5

Freefall had large zeppelins, even huge ones for cargo and large numbers of crew, but the four-passenger was the smallest we had. Woven wicker and bamboo formed the walls. Thin foam pads covered in blue cotton were tied to the wicker seats to provide a small amount of protection. The zeppelin had round portholes almost large enough to stick my head through, but the wicker covers were pulled tight, leaving the gondola lit only with the sunlight that seeped between the weave.

I'd lost lunch and missed dinner, so my stomach threatened to implode my abdomen any time now. A kind word to the canteen staff got me a box dinner, fried chicken with an extra serving of roasted potatoes and slaw. Normally I wouldn't touch anything that greasy and heavy, but I felt ready to eat a camel if anyone had one handy. Duffel bag in one hand, boxed dinner in the other, I ducked my head to get through the hatch and discovered Takamoto and Cedar, sitting side by side in the front of the gondola, facing the rear door.

"What are you doing here?" I blurted.

I shouldn't have been surprised. When you don't have wireless networks, when you don't have implants or datalinks, when you don't even have computers, the fastest communication you have is gossip. And we got by on raw gossip for hundreds of thousands of years.

Takamoto said, "Someone has to tell the rest of the team about Devin."

"We heard about the emergency zeppelin," Cedar said. "It had space, and—well, telling Kirk and George and Lyssa won't get any easier tomorrow."

I should have told Forecourt I wanted a private zeppelin. Getting information out of this morning's passengers would be difficult enough without the Diffusion team so upset. With my luck, though, Forecourt would have told me to take a floater. *Just fly straight into the sun, you can't miss it.*

I shifted my way through the hatch. The floor hardly gave at all underfoot. I tried not to think about what would—or, more precisely, wouldn't—be beneath us once we took off, and tried to make myself comfortable in one of the remaining chairs. The bottom felt comfortable, but the back only came up to the bottom of my shoulder blades. A rack of glass eye goggles with silk straps hung on one wall. The cozy space smelled of bamboo and wood polish, with a growing note of fried chicken that my stomach threatened to lunge at. "No cargo?" I said.

"We have clean uniforms on the Hindenbarge," Takamoto said.

So, Doctor, you do *know the word 'the.'* "They let you have the weight?"

Cedar said, "They have cargo steel out there. Thirty pounds of personal effects for each of us isn't a big deal. And that's Facility pounds, not Hindenbarge pounds."

An older man with a mustache you could sweep floors with stuck his head in the hatchway. "You Miss Redding?"

"Yes."

His lip curled. "Good. Welcome aboard the *Tahiti Sunset*. That makes you Cedar and… Takamoto."

Cedar nodded.

He knelt through the hatch and pulled the door shut behind him. "I'm Mitch MacConnor. You've been through the zeppelin passenger training, right?"

We all nodded.

"Well, too bad. You get a reminder now."

Cedar sighed. "We always do."

"And you always will," MacConnor said. "You each have a chute box under your seat. Get it out and put it on." He pointed at the harness he wore. "Straps under the groin, around the waist, over the shoulders."

The chute box was about the size of a thick paper equipment manual, but lighter than it seemed it should be. Takamoto and I had no trouble slipping into the silk straps and fastening the bamboo buckles, but Cedar had to crouch to keep her head from the wicker ceiling.

"These are self-folding, self-expanding chutes," MacConnor said intently.

"Yes, we know," Takamoto said.

MacConnor glared at Takamoto. "Pay attention again. You are about to go thirty kilometers in a wicker basket. A wicker basket designed to break apart."

I blinked. "Excuse me—break apart?" My voice didn't quite squeak.

MacConnor grinned. "They don't put it that way in training, do they? No, it's all 'in case of emergency.' Well, let me tell you. We can't trust structural steel out at the Hindenbarge, so the zeppelins are structural bamboo. Under a silk hot air bag." He cupped his hands together at right angles as if cradling a small bird. "If something goes wrong, if the bag blows, do you want everyone trying to fit out that little hatch? Or would you rather the cabin—" He gently let his hands come apart, opening them wide. "—clam-shell apart, nice and smooth?"

"If that happens," he continued, "steer yourself clear of the debris. You had the parachute training, back on Earth?"

"Sure." I'd enjoyed it. Even the part when they said *Now fall five thousand feet before opening your chute, and steer yourself left and right.* Each time I'd felt exhilarated from the moment I jumped, to when I again touched ground, all the way through dinner with my class afterwards.

"These chutes aren't floaters," MacConnor said. "But they're big. You get out from under the debris before you open up, and they'll slow you right the hell down, what with the upbreeze. And they stand out on radar. A blimp burst will get every radar on both sides screaming. You'll have zeppelins on you in less than an hour. You won't drop a kilometer." He eyed me up and down. "Small as you are, you might even rise a little. Whatever you do, don't steer. Steering makes you drop faster, so you leave the pedals alone. Let the zeppelins come to you."

"But that hasn't happened," I said.

"Not for, oh, must be two years now," MacConnor's mustache grinned. "Hey, girl, don't look like that. The bag blows, the clamshell dumps you clear instantly. It's all mechanical. This stuff works, or I wouldn't do it. Montague pays good, but my hide is worth more than that."

"Right," I said.

"You just keep that chute box on," MacConnor said. "It's amazing stuff. Light, strong, made out of omnifold fiber. Those things can be used a million times and they'll still work just like new. And they're reflective—they stand out against the red for three or four kilometers. Human terminal velocity without the chute is about eleven hundred kilometers an hour, but so long as you have a chute box, you'll be fine."

Cedar said "We've had someone on every flight since the Hindenbarge opened. Everybody's come back safe."

"Vell," Takamoto said, "Marcus *did* hurt leg when clamshell—"

Cedar elbowed his ribs, not gently.

MacConnor double-checked the latch behind him. "Just to be safe, buckle in." He grabbed the ladder to the pilot's loft. "I'll leave the roof hatch open so you can hear me, but it's not an invite. You want a view, open a window."

"Relax," Cedar said. "It's fine. Sit down and eat your dinner, you look like you're starving."

I plopped back into my seat, staring at the box of fried chicken. "You know, I don't think I'm hungry anymore."

6

The wicker basket swayed gently around me, tickling primordial sense memories of rocking in a cradle or in my mother's arms. My abandoned dinner's aroma faded, leaving the scents of clean polished wood laced with machine oil and dust. The zeppelin's old-fashioned electrical drive ran even quieter than the whoosh of the great bamboo fans it drove.

Leaning my shoulders against the woven wall, head back, eyes closed, I tried to rest my tired eyes and aching head. I'd awoken at six AM, and it would be nine PM before the zeppelin hit the Hindenbarge. If the passengers from this morning's flight were awake and available, I had more hours of talking to them before I could sleep. I needed to conserve energy, especially my mental energy. And every time my mind strayed to what lay beneath us, I had to remind myself that we weren't that far up, and if we had trouble the zeppelin could just gently ease itself to the ground.

I am total crap at lying to myself.

By shifting around, I found a spot where the wicker ends didn't gouge my scalp and shoulder too badly, so long as I kept my weight on them. The only sounds were the whirring of the blades, wind softly whistling through the weave, and Cedar's and Takamoto's quiet whispers.

Maybe I fell asleep.

A distant voice shouted, then Cedar said "Redding? You awake?"

"She's asleep," Takamoto said.

I heaved my head upright, trying to ignore the stale taste of my mouth. "No," I yawned, "I'm up."

"Goggles," Takamoto said. "On the wall, by your seat."

"You'll want to see this," Cedar said.

My back muscles ached as I fumbled for the goggles. Our basket swayed and rocked, and my stomach rolled with it.

I barely had the smoked glass goggles over my eyes when Cedar swung aside a panel in the basket's front wall. A three-foot glassless window framed the Hindenbarge.

Imagine the most monstrously huge balloon you've ever seen.

Now imagine dozens of them, hundreds, all clustered together like grapes. Platforms hung beneath the balloons, all different shapes and sizes: some cubes, some flat boxes, some dangling lines and derricks. Lines and cables and scaffolds connected the whole assembly.

One of the suns hung right behind the Hindenbarge, silhouetting the whole thing in fuming reds and oranges. The dangling platforms and bulging air sacs cast shadows kilometers deep.

Takamoto grinned at my expression. "Impressive, *da*?"

I couldn't figure out its size. Without any ground, without any clouds, without being able to see any humanizing details, I couldn't process its scale.

The zeppelin's bamboo prop blades whooshed overhead just as much as ever, pushing us through the endless sky. Wind through the window ruffled my hair back. And the Hindenbarge didn't grow any bigger.

"They keep adding to it," Cedar said. "Earth wants all the molecular-diffused steel they can get."

"How big is that?" I asked.

"One thousand seven hundred meters, end-to-end," Takamoto said. "All genetically engineered structural bamboo."

Behind the smoked glasses I blinked. "There's really no metal out there?"

I realized my mistake half a second too late. Never ask a specialist about their field unless you're hoping they'll handle both sides of the conversation for you.

Takamoto straightened his back and actually reached for the suspenders he didn't have on. "Freefall has scalar matter coherence. Out there," he waved, "steel grows weak. Ten kilometers further in—*if* you go quickly enough, it diffuses. Expands." He formed an inflating balloon with his hands. "And we, we mathematically predict diffusion patterns."

"It works the same the other way," Cedar said. "Dig into the cliff, and everything gets more solid. Everything more than two klicks deep is solid neutronium. They—"

"They are nothing," Takamoto said. "They try for *years* to dig neutronium. They get nothing! Never will. But out here? My team? A rod like this," Takamoto said, holding his hands about a foot apart, "cut just right, it inflates—*pow*!—into I-beam. I-beam stronger than plain beam, and weighs *seven kilos*. On Earth!"

"I'd like to see that," I said.

Cedar said "The—"

"So would we all," Takamoto said over her, oblivious to Cedar's sudden glare. "Two kilometer past the Hindenbarge, your body come apart. Is also mathematically predictable. You look like squidodactyl. We use dirigibles, bamboo clockwork, to control the steel diffusers."

Takamoto burbled on, while I sat back in my chair and stared at the slowly growing platform.

I'd seen diffused steel before. Everyone on Freefall had. But I hadn't appreciated how we made it until I saw the Hindenbarge. It looked too big to be real. And it couldn't be real, on Earth.

We'd built a wonder in the sky.

In another universe's sky.

This was why I'd joined Montague. If it meant I had to help scrape some poor bastard off the Debris Shield, it was totally worth it.

One of the smaller balloons moved independently. I blinked, and suddenly my eyes made sense of them. That balloon was a zeppelin, one of the huge cargo zeppelins, with bundles of diffused steel dangling from its belly. It swam past us like a whale ignoring a flounder, but up in the minuscule perch for the pilot I made out a speck waving at us.

That zeppelin was bigger than all of the Facility. It would dock far below the floors where we ate and worked, offloading cargo to be lugged through the Portal back to Earth.

"You have to be careful," Cedar said. "If you cut the stock wrong, it'll diffuse badly. Nobody wants an I-beam with sharp edges, it'll have your arm off before you notice. We have a few of the really good ones back in the office."

"They have to be at office," Takamoto said. "Leave steel here more than a week, it gets weak. Diffusion needs speed. Out here, just—" he shrugged "—rots."

"The people trying to dig far enough into the cliff to get neutronium have been at it for ten years now," Cedar said. "Our department's profits have covered the last eight of that, and projects in a dozen other universes too."

MacConnor brought us to the Hindenbarge so smoothly I hardly knew we'd connected. One moment our basket swayed, then the motion stopped. I let out a deep breath and unbuckled.

"Careful!" MacConnor said, dropping through the ceiling hatch. He came down the ladder using only his hands, letting his feet swing free into the room. "If *I* weigh twenty kilos here, Miss Redding, *you* weigh about a sneeze."

I stopped, then carefully undid the belt.

Cedar unbuckled, laid her forearm over her head to protect it from the ceiling, then stood. I followed her example, and rose so quickly that my feet left the ground. My forearm was squeezed between my head and the ceiling, and then I settled back down.

"Light steps," MacConnor said. "You'll get it."

My duffel bag weighted less than one of the boots I'd left in my quarters.

MacConnor untied the rear hatch and held it open for me. "Thank you for flying *Tahiti Sunset* airlines."

I followed MacConnor out onto the dock.

The basket sat on an enclosed platform of structural bamboo. The zeppelin's glowing underbelly formed the ceiling, glowing in white and pink from diffused light. Sunlight streamed through gaps between the bamboo struts behind us, and the breeze carried hot metal and burning wood.

A man loomed on the platform, wearing a Montague Security uniform with the blue epaulets of a Second. His chin looked like it could do double duty as a plow and his eyes shone with energy, but stubble darkened his face and he'd combed his dark brown hair with his fingers.

"Security Third Redding," he said in a voice like a rock crusher, stepping forward and holding out his right hand.

"Mister Lundbaugh, sir?" I reached to take his hand.

He harrumphed. "You have a message from your supervisor, I *hope*."

"Oh!" I jerked my hand back and fumbled in my pockets. The white envelope from Forecourt was in my right thigh pocket, slightly bent but still sealed.

Lundbaugh took it from me impatiently, tore it open with a thumb. His bushy eyebrows crawled closer together as he read. "I was ready for bed."

"Sorry, sir," I said.

Cedar waved one hand in farewell as she and Takamoto slipped out a side door. MacConnor had already vanished.

"So," he drawled. "You're here to talk to the morning zeppelin passengers. We start work early out here, but don't worry—I'll get them rousted for you."

The information I'd gathered earlier suddenly felt completely irrelevant. I'd made a huge deal out of this for nothing. Yes, I couldn't make sense of the facts, but someone smarter could. Gupper had died of misadventure, a normal ordinary misadventure. He must have. Pushing any other explanation would only make me a bigger fool and wreck what little career I had. "It could wait for morning, sir."

"Oh, no!" Lundbaugh showed his teeth. It wasn't a smile. "We can't have anyone missing their flight back in the morning. If I'm up, *everyone's* up." He folded Forecourt's message into a neat square. "Besides, this might be a *serious* crime you're here about. It's not just an industrial accident. Got to take it *serious*. Urgent, even."

I wanted to slink away.

But, dammit, the facts *didn't* make sense.

"If the radio had worked," Lundbaugh said, "I could have saved you the trip. This morning's zeppelin arrived just fine. On time. They certainly didn't stop to—" he smirked "—throw anyone overboard."

7

The Hindenbarge had its own rhythm, a slower sway than the tiny zeppelin, a private tide formed of shifting silk and flexing bamboo and creaking hemp, an inexorable inertia that you had to accept before you could walk. The platform's slow rotation skewed every movement: every dropped object landed just a little bit off target, every door closed a little too enthusiastically or lethargically. I found myself grateful for my gum-soled shoes, offering me a little extra traction on bamboo decks and ladders even while reduced weight nibbled at friction.

But I got answers.

The morning zeppelin—yesterday morning's zeppelin, by the time I finished—had a completely uneventful flight. Nobody on the flight had seen Devin Gupper. They hadn't detoured above the Debris Shield.

At almost one in the morning, I released tired and confused scientists and mechanics to the custody of their beds. When I told Lundbaugh I'd finished, he huffed and scowled and pointed me to a hammock. My pilot was asleep, returning to the Facility didn't demand urgency, and the *Tahiti Sunset* had to recharge for the journey home anyway. Zeppelins could only do about forty kilometers on a charge.

The weave and tide of the Hindenbarge rocked me to dreamless sleep.

A support clerk shook me awake too soon to tell me that the *Tahiti Sunset* would leave for the Facility in half an hour. He brought me a sandwich, a cup of coffee, and a sealed envelope from Lundbaugh, for Forecourt.

I made it to the dock with four minutes to spare. Cedar was already there, an Irish warrior from before the Oil Age, trying not to catch her red hair in the wicker ceiling and looking even more bleary-eyed than I felt. "Doctor Cedar," I said.

She nodded. "Redding. How was your trip?"

Useless and stupid. "Necessary." I strapped the chute box onto my back and took my seat. Last night's boxed dinner still sat on the floor, its fried chicken and potatoes and butter certainly congealed and festering. I'd have to remember to take it out when I left. "How was yours?"

Cedar heaved out a breath. "Rough. Everybody—" Her voice cracked. She took a moment to steady herself and said, "Everybody liked Devin. I mean, he was a good guy. Not one of those people with a rough outside but they're okay when you get to know them. I mean, he honestly gave a damn. He wanted everyone to be successful. Did you know he wrote half a dozen Diffusion monographs, but he made sure he wasn't the only one listed as author? Kirk can't write a grocery list without doing thirty drafts to try to make it coherent, but he's a hell of a mathematician. Devin made sure he got credit on every single paper based on his work, though."

"He sounds like a decent guy," I said.

"He was."

Takamoto stuck his head in the door. "Good morning."

"Doctor," I said.

"Miss Redding. You have good trip?"

"I did what I had to do."

"And Lucy," Takamoto said. "How are you today?"

Cedar shrugged. Devin's death had hit her hard.

My trip hadn't been wasted, I told myself. A negative result is still a result. And Gupper's death still didn't make sense. How had he gotten up high enough to die splattered across the Debris Shield?

And I knew too many Montague scientists who would steal every scrap of credit they could get in hope of being assigned more glamorous problems. Freefall was one of Montague's successes, but not much in the way of cutting-edge research happened there beyond the ongoing failure of the neutronium project. Gupper sounded like a rare creature, one worth keeping.

MacConnor came in, took us through the pre-flight instruction, and we set out for the Facility, the cliff, and solid ground. After the Hindenbarge's majestic tides, the rocking of the *Tahiti Sunset*'s rickety basket dangling beneath the silk hot air bag unnerved me even more than it had on the flight out. Although I hadn't eaten, my lurching stomach dissuaded me from testing the sandwich.

I closed my eyes and focused on the facts of Gupper's death rather than the endless emptiness beneath.

Devin Gupper had fallen to his death on the Debris Shield. I made myself review his impact, trying to set aside the blood and broken bone and visualize how he'd hit. He'd landed almost perpendicular to the cliff, his head about a meter from the granite, arms outstretched in a Y. The impact had been so hard he'd deformed, his torso flattening, body bulging out at the sides, the front of his skull destroyed. The corpse slid half a meter down, until a gum-soled shoe and a sleeve had caught on separate rivets.

I must have chewed that image for half an hour as the dirigible slid through the sky at a breakneck thirty kilometers an hour, trying to make sense of it. He'd fallen out of the sky, somehow, and hit at an incredible speed.

Cedar and Takamoto spent the time arguing about rescheduling work assignments. I got the impression that Takamoto was trying to give Cedar something more immediate to focus on, instead of Gupper's death.

"I think you should give Marcus a chance with the titanium diffusion," Cedar said.

Eleven hundred kilometers an hour was terminal velocity for a human being in freefall on Freefall. How far would you have to fall to reach that speed? I'd have to figure it out sometime.

"Marcus is good," Takamoto said, "but I really need him on the coupler math."

How long would it take someone to fall that distance?

What did Gupper think as he fell?

"The coupler project is really straightforward," Cedar said. "I mean, it's almost a waste of his time."

Everyone did parachute and free-fall training before coming to Freefall. With enough distance, Gupper could have steered himself away from the Debris Shield.

"Is easy income," Takamoto said.

Had Gupper aimed himself at the Debris Shield?

"It's not all about income," Cedar said.

Maybe I should get MacConnor to take a detour. We could go up the cliff above the Debris Shield. Surely MacConnor knew how far someone would have to fall to hit that hard.

"Is all about income," Takamoto said. "We make Freefall even more profitable, we choose next assignment. I help you myself."

MacConnor had a certain flair to him. Maybe I should see if he wanted to get dinner tonight.

"Devin and I had that project for two years," Cedar said. "I'm not letting you swoop in at the end and grab credit."

But MacConnor's mustache, it could double as a paintbrush.

"Devin will get full credit," Takamoto said. "Is smallest we can do. You look through his papers. See what he did not finish. Team will split up, he gets credit on all he touched. He has two boys on Earth, they can use royalties."

The pilots probably had rules against diverting without letting either the Facility or the Hindenbarge know. We should probably dock first. Let Cedar and Takamoto off, let MacConnor file a flight plan, then the two of us could go up and look at the cliff.

Cedar sighed. "Sorry, I didn't mean to snap like that. It's just…"

No, I needed to check in with Forecourt. That would not be fun.

"Is hard," Takamoto said quietly. "Is hard for us all."

If I wanted to look at the cliff over the Debris Shield, Forecourt would probably tell me to take a floater. The thought made my stomach clench like a fist. I'd have something under me the whole way—the Debris Shield. I'd only stood on the Shield once, so that wasn't a pleasant thought.

Cedar and Takamoto were quiet for a moment.

Either my pride or my dignity was done. I'd ask for MacConnor to take me up in the *Tahiti Sunset*. And it had nothing to do with MacConnor, he was just the only pilot I knew and I didn't want to throw up while riding a floater.

But that mustache.

"If we really want to push on titanium diffusion," Cedar said, "maybe we can get someone to take care of the neutronium calculations they have me doing."

I couldn't help imagining my own puke spattering on the Debris Shield. At terminal velocity.

"*Da*," Takamoto said. "I try again. As soon as I finish payroll today, I help you."

My pulse suddenly thrummed in my temples.

Adrenaline surged in my veins.

This is not the place.

My head wanted to jerk up, but I made it stay still. I didn't even breathe deeply or let my eyes open.

We hung in a rickety wicker basket dangling over infinity. I don't care how well a wicker basket is made—if you're suspended from a balloon over a literally bottomless drop, it's rickety.

But Doctor Cedar, too smart for her own good, said "Payroll was due yesterday, though."

"Payroll? *Da*, payroll," Takamoto said. He spoke too quickly. "I mean other paperwork."

My shoulders wanted to rise, but I forced them to remain still. Accept that, Cedar. Do not argue here, in a picnic basket, dangling over forever.

"You always said payroll was last," Cedar said. Her voice turned suspicious. "What were you *really* doing yesterday morning?"

"What are you implying?" Takamoto said.

Crap. I opened my eyes and slowly sat up, as if awakening again. "Sorry, I must have drifted off." Maybe that would cool off the discussion.

Takamoto's face burned bright red. He glared at Cedar.

Cedar didn't flinch.

For a moment we sat there, three figurines in a basket.

Then Cedar looked at me and said, "Doctor Takamoto lied about where he was when Devin disappeared."

Takamoto said "Unacceptable!" He wrenched off his seat belt and flung it aside. The buckle bounced harmlessly off Cedar's thigh. "I do not have to sit here and take accusation from subordinate!"

"Wait," I said. "Hang on, let's talk this out." One hand went to my own safety belt. I didn't want to fire my taser sitting down. The *Tahiti Sunset*'s cramped basket was no place to subdue someone, but I'd need all the maneuverability I could get.

Takamoto said "I will not be accused!"

Cedar said "I just asked—"

Takamoto whirled and grabbed the ladder leading to the pilot's loft.

"Takamoto, no!" I said flinging my own belt aside.

Takamoto scrambled up the ladder and out the loft hatch.

Cedar looked at me, brows furrowed beneath her shocking red hair.

MacConnor shouted something angry, but the wind carried away his words.

I grabbed the ladder, leaned close to Cedar, and stage-whispered, "Don't have this fight here. Apologize. Wait for us to land."

Her frown intensified, then understanding lit her face as she touched the wicker wall next to her.

I nodded, then hoisted myself up a rung on the ladder.

MacConnor's next shout carried naked rage.

I scuttled up two bamboo rungs, grabbed the edges of the hatch, and heaved myself up just in time for MacConnor to collapse on top of me.

Blood smeared across my face.

8

I stood on the bamboo ladder at the hatch for half a second, paralyzed.

MacConnor had toppled on top of me, his chest smashing against the crown of my head and crushing me back down the ladder. We were about halfway between the Hindenbarge and the Facility, but he weighed more than I could lift with my neck.

My hands were still above the hatch, where I'd been about to hoist myself into the pilot's nest. I flailed out, stretching, trying to grab something, anything. The bamboo deck slipped across my fingertips, then my left hand caught a gap. I dug my fingers between bamboo strips to anchor myself to the top of the ladder.

Sticky blood covered my forehead, my cheek. The smell of copper filled my nose. My stomach clenched even harder.

Beneath me, inside the zeppelin's tiny wicker passenger space, Cedar shouted in surprise.

MacConnor's chest heaved.

The whole zeppelin shuddered and twitched around us, stressing every fragile connection. Structural bamboo—a total contradiction. This was a ramshackle deathtrap, and our pilot was bleeding, maybe dying.

Gripping my unseen anchor more tightly, I heaved myself up. MacConnor cried out in pain, then rolled to the side. My head emerged into open air.

The pilot's loft hung in the breezy open space of Freefall, a complex nest of silk cables and bamboo struts connecting the passenger basket to the huge red-and-white air bag overhead. I blinked at the column of sinking suns, their majestic descent in reds and oranges coloring the whole sky.

Something liquid oozed down to my upper lip. I tasted fresh blood.

Takamoto stood beside the pilot's console. One hand held a length of shining metal no larger than a pen, with a line of blood slipping down its bottom side and dripping to the floor. His round face looked blank, and his jaw flapped helplessly.

MacConnor deserved better, but I set my shoulder against his side and tried to heave him aside so I could squeeze out. His cry of pain had no thought behind it, just the blind mewling of a helpless animal.

I almost had MacConnor out of the way when Takamoto saw me. "No!"

I got another shoulder past MacConnor and tried to pull that arm up after it.

Takamoto lunged forward, the shining steel in his hand arcing through the air.

Instinctively, I flinched aside, my feet kicking, trying to squirm my way through the hatch.

The knife plunged through my outstretched, anchoring hand.

The blade punched through the back of my palm into the deck like hot ice, sinking effortlessly between the bones of my hand and into the bamboo deck. My nerves flared, outraged agony crashing up my arm into my whole body.

They tell you in training not to pull at a puncture like a knife. They don't tell you that if your hand gets nailed to the deck, ancient animal instincts will make you recoil. I reflexively pulled myself back, wanting to shut everything down and coil myself around this fresh hot agony in my hand, not even thinking about being nailed to the deck.

The blade slid effortlessly through the pinky edge of my hand, slicing bone and muscle and sinew as cleanly as a surgical laser or an axe.

I screamed and fell back, grabbing at my bisected hand, tumbling back into the wicker passenger basket, slashing my head against the edge of a chair before my back bounced off another chair and I rolled to the ground, a tight knot of horrified pain.

Cedar screamed.

MacConnor's head and upper torso filled the hatch, suspended by his chute box caught on the edge. The chute box *thunked* with the kick that knocked it free, and the burly pilot fell headfirst to the floor behind me.

Takamoto's round face, bright red, eyes broad in panic, filled the hatch for a moment. Then the hatch slapped shut.

The latch rasped.

9

My brain quit.

My left hand was cut through like someone had plunged a power saw into the edge halfway between the base of the pinky and my wrist, and whacked through to the very edge of my index finger. Blood pulsed from the gap, drenching everything. The pain disappeared against the absolute horror of the wound, a violation exposing things never meant to see light.

I'm pretty sure I screamed. A lot.

Then Cedar grabbed me, shouting "Redding! Aidan!"

Pain started returning like the early hints of an onrushing tide. I knew Cedar was there, but somehow she wasn't important. Only my hand mattered, holding it still, protecting it so I could scream.

Then Cedar grabbed my wrist.

I thrashed, knowing that nobody should touch that intimate maiming.

Cedar sat on my chest, trapping my arm between her thighs.

I bucked ineffectively.

She wrenched at my hand.

I shrieked.

The pain evaporated, ending as cleanly as turning off the lights.

Cut free from that white-hot cold agony, I passed out.

10

Consciousness oozed back a moment or two later. I had curled protectively around my maimed hand, but not so desperately.

A thick white cotton patch covered my wound, curving around the blade edge of my hand. It looked like a sponge, somehow taping me together despite the fresh sticky blood sheeting my hand and arm.

Cedar. The first-aid kit.

She'd kept her head, grabbed the trauma patches, and glued me together. The drugs would keep my hand desensitized for a few more hours, encourage healing, and help me stave off infection. We didn't have nanobot meds on Freefall, but if we could get back to Medical soon I might not even lose that half of my hand—I'd made it to twenty-six without needing anything regrown, and I had really hoped to keep that streak going to twenty-seven.

MacConnor lay on the wicker deck, his feet next to me and his head up against the front. We barely had enough room for the two of us to sprawl out in the zeppelin's passenger compartment. Cedar had ripped off his shirt. She'd already slapped a trauma patch, one of the smaller ones, on his gut, and was sizing a paper-wrapped patch against the bloody gash in his chest.

The basket lurched.

Overhead, Takamoto swore.

The hatch remained closed.

"Cedar," I said. My voice rasped in my dry throat. "Next size up. Multiple injuries need extra meds. Avoid shock."

She glanced back at me. "Right, forgot." She tossed the patch back in the first aid kit, grabbed one the size of a dinner plate, and tore it open. "Never had to really do this." She pressed the patch over the wound. "You can't overdose on trauma patches, can you?"

With my uninjured hand I grabbed the edge of a seat and pulled myself upright. Wicker scratches marred my face, my own blood drenched my arm and chest, MacConnor's blood smeared my face, and somewhere in this I'd twisted my back.

I lurched like a broken machine.

But I moved.

I rubbed my aching shoulder with my remaining hand. "That's a good armbar you have there."

Cedar flashed me a quick grin.

MacConnor groaned.

"That should hold him," Cedar said. She frowned. "It's all I've got, anyway." Her voice grew quiet. "He used diffused steel, that stuff cuts you like—" She glanced at me. "Uh, it's bad."

I nodded. MacConnor looked like he was breathing a little more easily, and color started edging back into him. He had some impressive pecs, despite all the hair—

Pull it together, Redding. Yes, you're hurt, you could have been killed, you're having a nice post-not-dead hormone rush. Enjoy it later. But if you don't take charge of this zeppelin, if you don't get a handle on Takamoto, this can go even worse.

I clambered to my feet. I'd wrenched my hip, too. My head whirled for a second, then my balance steadied. "Let me get past." I sucked in another breath. "Ladder."

Cedar glanced up. "You're in no shape to climb."

The zeppelin lurched again. Bamboo creaked.

She was right. I'd lost blood—it covered me, the floor, a seat cushion, and Cedar. I kept sucking air to try to make up the lack. My body struggled to keep me upright. The drugs shut off the pain, but the shock of the trauma still made my grip weak and my vision shaky. I needed to lie down.

"And Takamoto clearly doesn't know how to fly this thing," I said. "Someone's got to talk him down before he gets us all killed. Have *you* been through hostile negotiations training?"

Cedar gritted her teeth and shifted herself so I could squeeze past.

Hostile negotiations training? Yeah, that's what they call it when another student pretends to be a bomber and you talk her down. Or the AI-driven gunman in virtual. It's not when you're locked inside a giant picnic basket dangling over infinity and hanging from a balloon driven by a desperate, irrational mathematician trying to slash his way out of his problems.

Keeping my maimed hand over my heart, I climbed the ladder one-handed. The basket lurched and swayed, but we still weren't back at full weight and I clutched my way to the top. Once my head brushed the closed access hatch I shouted "Doctor Takamoto!"

The basket lurched again. I heard Takamoto cry out. What was he doing up there? It's not like there were speed bumps out here. You aimed at the cliff and waited.

"Listen to me, Takamoto!" What was his first name again? "Haider! It's not too late. We can work this out! Whatever's going on, whatever you've done, we can talk about it."

The whole zeppelin creaked.

I thought of trying the "there's no place to go" gambit, but Takamoto wasn't thinking well. I didn't want him puncturing the air bag as a final, futile gesture.

"I'm okay," I shouted. "MacConnor will be too, if we get back soon. You've done nothing permanent here! Just let us up so we can talk this out!"

Bamboo creaked.

Then snapped.

The basket's rear end sagged, turning my nice vertical ladder into a set of rungs across an angled ceiling. My hand clamped weakly on a rung, but my feet instantly slipped free. I shouted wordlessly and, for the second time in ten minutes, fell backwards to the floor and slid to the back wall.

Cedar screamed, this time with full unchecked terror, clutching her seat.

MacConnor slid down the short aisle, his feet crashing into me, his body crumpling after them.

More bamboo creaked.

I tried to shove MacConnor aside. Again.

Takamoto shouted "Lucy!"

The knife. The diffused steel knife that had cut through my hand.

How long would it take that knife to cut through structural bamboo?

"Haider!" Cedar screamed. "Stop this!"

"I would have," Takamoto said. "I would have done anything for you."

Wood snapped and groaned.

Then the *Tahiti Sunset*'s passenger basket plummeted into infinity.

11

Falling.

Everything in the passenger basket became weightless. Doctor Cedar came off her chair, red hair rising into an electric halo, highlighting her high-pitched shriek of absolute terror. Last night's boxed dinner bounced off the back of a seat and careened towards the ceiling. The creaking of bamboo was replaced by wind whistling through the warp and weft of the weave. I thrashed, and MacConnor's limp form rose into the air.

Clamshell.

The basket was going to split in half, spilling us into empty air.

MacConnor still wore his chute box, but an unconscious person can't pull a trigger. I pawed at his leg, but the fingers of my left hand wouldn't even try to close. Desperately I snatched his belt with my working right hand. When the basket split open, I'd have to get us both free, trigger his chute, and then trigger my own.

How long would the clamshell take to open?

Cedar grabbed a seat to anchor herself.

The basket twitched and started rolling.

The wind rushed faster, whistling through the weave, suspending us inside the basket.

Come on, open! I wanted to beat at the wall, but the bandage on my free hand stopped me.

"Too long," Cedar shouted. "It's taking too long!"

The passenger compartment should clamshell open. It's automatic, a mechanism—

—but *where* was that mechanism?

Probably up in all that machinery and struts and entanglements surrounding the pilot's perch.

The passenger compartment wasn't going to open.

We had to get out ourselves.

I fought to shove the fear aside. My heart surged in my chest.

The pilot's hatch was the closest exit. I kicked off the wall, dragging MacConnor with me. *Get him out. Get myself out. Pull his chute, then mine. And Cedar.*

Or I'd spend the rest of my life falling.

And my entire death, too.

Forever.

The basket continued its own slow rotation, but my head had its own countering spin. I'd lost blood.

One working hand. I pried my hands from MacConnor's belt and fumbled at the door.

Hyperventilating. I forced my breathing slower and deeper. *Think, Redding!*

We fell at one gravity. Ten meters per second per second.

After falling one minute, we'd be going three hundred meters a second. That had to be above terminal velocity?

The emptiness was swallowing us. My every muscle trembled, but I wrenched at the hatch.

It wouldn't open.

The wind through the turning wicker rasped my face.

Wait—Takamoto had locked this hatch. I cursed myself for twelve kinds of fool.

MacConnor had drifted towards the floor. I kicked down towards him, only to collide with Cedar as she tried to get to the rear hatch. We bounced off each other into the churning chaos of the tumbling, turning passenger compartment.

Eleven hundred kilometers an hour. Terminal velocity. About three hundred meters a second.

I clutched at something, trying to anchor myself. A chute box, knocked from its place beneath a seat.

A scream bulged up my throat. I clamped down on it.

My foot hit something, but by the time I could turn to look, it was gone. My back bounced off a wall.

The passenger compartment spun faster.

Dread threatened to burst my heart, my ribs, my skull.

Three hundred meters a second. Eighteen kilometers a minute.

How long had it been since we fell?

Zeppelins had a range of forty kilometers.

Either we escaped this tumbling madhouse in two minutes, or we fell forever.

I lashed out my good hand and seized a wicker chair back as it spun past. It wrenched itself out of my hand, leaving torn skin and welling fresh blood.

I tumbled away.

The heel of a shoe rushed towards my face.

The flailing foot crashed into my temple.

Blackness.

12

I came back resting against a wall.

The passenger cabin had stopped its mad tumble. What had been a wall was a ceiling, with a half-meter porthole hanging open exposing the red sky. Cedar huddled next to me, while MacConnor lay akimbo on my other side.

We were still falling.

The wind through the gaps in the wicker screeched and whistled, buffeting my short hair into a cloud at the top and sides of my vision.

I was weightless, held to the floor only by Cedar's light touch.

Complete freefall.

The terror had collapsed, leaving me strangely numb. We were falling. We would fall forever. Our last meal would be whatever we could scrounge from this empty wicker basket.

I raised my head. Cedar had tears in her eyes, but the wind shredded them before they could trail down her cheeks.

How long had it been? I raised my aching arm to glance at my watch, remembered when we'd left, and did the math.

Takamoto had cut us free about ten minutes ago.

A hundred and eighty kilometers above.

I would die, here, with Cedar and MacConnor. My new best friends.

Every muscle in me ached. My unarmed combat training had included bare-knuckles brawling, but the bruises and bludgeoning I'd suffered from then didn't come close to the no-holds-barred battering I'd taken from the tumbling basket. My maimed hand felt like a numb balloon, somehow larger than the rest of me.

I let my good hand fumble for Cedar's. She clasped it tightly. Her fingers shook for a moment, then were still.

"How'd you stop the roll?" I shouted above the roaring wind.

Cedar gave a thin, brave smile. Her red hair floated above her, blown by the wind into a shifting grass rising from her scalp. "I knocked the hatch open. The extra airflow changed the aerodynamics enough that we straightened out."

If anything, the wicker felt more stable than it had before. Everything felt light and smooth. The air almost supported me.

Freefall had no weather beyond the constant slow rise of warm air. The basket wasn't fighting through the air any more; it flowed with it.

Even my teeth hurt.

Surrender felt easy. Not only was there no way to fight, fighting this couldn't accomplish anything. We were falling. We would always fall. Even if Montague expanded their operations downward, the Facility couldn't grow at terminal velocity.

I was going to die.

I squeezed Cedar's hand, and felt her squeeze back.

But I couldn't give up. There was no way to fight death? Fine. I would figure out *why*.

Takamoto had lied about doing payroll yesterday. He'd been willing to kill us to keep that secret.

What secret was worth killing over? Killing Gupper was the obvious answer.

"Cedar," I shouted.

"Call me Lucy," she said.

I smiled back. "Then it's Aidan. Listen—when did you get to the lab yesterday morning? What time?"

"About eight. Why?"

"Takamoto was there all day?"

"All the time I was."

Gupper had been seen right before seven. So, in an hour, Takamoto had killed Gupper, then somehow gotten his body up above the Debris Shield. Way above the Shield, judging from the damage done to his body. He couldn't have taken a floater that high and returned in an hour, especially lugging Gupper's body.

Gupper struck the Debris Shield at four thirty PM. Hours and hours later. While Takamoto was in the lab, with his staff.

And Takamoto wasn't a calm, methodical killer. Standing in the pilot's perch, he'd been almost paralyzed while I tried to climb out. He panicked. He wouldn't have set up something in advance to take Gupper up to the Shield.

So how could Gupper have gotten up there?

An answer exploded in the back of my brain, and my eyes snapped open. I found myself sitting up, heedless of my injuries, mouth working soundlessly.

"What is it?" Cedar said.

The idea was insane.

It was ridiculous.

But it explained *everything*.

"I think… I think I might know how to save us," I said.

13

If I guessed wrong, we were dead.

If I was right but we screwed up, we were dead.

If we did nothing? Dead.

So we went for it.

Cedar—*Lucy*—and I pillaged the wicker passenger compartment, moving carefully. We weren't quite weightless in the plunging box, but the screaming hurricane updraft that made talking almost impossible buoyed us. Each touch made the passenger compartment wobble and shake in a threat to tumble again, but it never quite lost its new direction.

Smoked glass goggles—we'd need those. Bamboo-cased binoculars, meant for sightseeing. Lucy found half a dozen liter bottles of water in a locker woven into the wall. I grabbed a bottle and drained it, feeling my parched tissues soak up the fluid.

Then we took MacConnor's pants off.

Don't give me that look. We needed something to tie everything together with, and the passenger compartment didn't come with rope. And he lost the vote, two to one. So we stole MacConnor's pants and cut them into long strips. Lucy lashed the first-aid kit to her belt. I knotted the spare chute box to mine—I didn't have a plan for the chute box, but if we needed it, we'd *really* need it.

And MacConnor still had his boxers. Red ones.

I grabbed the white box containing last night's supper.

Lucy's face wrinkled. "You're not going to eat that!" she shouted over the roaring wind.

I shook my head. "Windburn!"

The fried chicken, and the butter on the potatoes, had all cooled and congealed into a greasy mess and tumbled. I dug my finger into a lump of alloyed grease and butter, took a deep breath to still my revulsion, and smeared it on my face.

Lucy made a face, nodded, and grabbed a greasy chicken breast.

We were able to cover our own face and hands, and used the rest slapdash on MacConnor's bare skin. There was an awful lot of him. We tied his torn shirt around his torso for more protection.

I took a few strips of MacConnor's torn pants and tied them together, forming a makeshift rope. I tied a slipknot in each end and put one around my right wrist, tugging it snug. The other end I looped around MacConnor's left wrist. Our ankles got the same treatment. Lucy mirrored me on MacConnor's other side.

Lucy's face gleamed pale beneath the speckles of greasy breading. "Are you sure about this, Aidan?"

"If you have a better idea," I said at the top of my lungs, "I'd really love to hear it."

Lucy took my good hand in hers. I squeezed. We grinned at each other. I hoped mine didn't look as maniacal as hers and tied the smoked-glass goggles over my eyes.

"Whatever happens, it's been a pleasure," I shouted.

"Don't say that. After we pull this off, we'll be invited to *all* the best parties."

I gave her a thumbs up and looked towards the entrance hatch on the wall.

We made our way to the entrance hatch, moving almost weightlessly, MacConnor's arms over our shoulders. Lucy looked like she could have carried MacConnor on her own. If MacConnor fell on me, though, I might smother before Lucy could rescue me.

We braced our feet on the seats and pressed our shoulders against the wall around the hatch.

I clenched MacConnor to my side with my good hand, and felt Lucy respond in kind.

Then Lucy yanked the hatch open.

The passenger cabin immediately whirled, wrenching all of us around. I held my spot, pinning my body between the seat and the wall with the strength of my legs and back. My bruised legs burned, but I held my place.

The basket steadied, wobbled, and stabilized, with the exit hatch in the ceiling. Freefall's aerodynamics, its unnatural natural laws, apparently demanded that the passenger cabinet's largest hole be at the top. That was one right guess, thankfully.

Cedar climbed through the door first, towing MacConnor after her.

The cotton leashes tied to my good wrist and ankle tugged, then pulled. Before they could grow more taut, I ducked my head out the hatch and shimmered out after them.

My feet cleared the hole.

We were free.

The passenger compartment rose above us, and we fell into hazy red oblivion.

14

The screaming air cradled me like an impossibly comfortable bed. Air shrieked past me far more loudly than it had skydiving on Earth, but caressed me aloft. I felt utterly weightless.

If it weren't for the part where we were falling at eleven hundred kilometers an hour, I'd almost enjoy this.

Lucy and I settled out facing the falling suns, a column of smoking red orbs that began impossibly far overhead and descended into infinity, casting amber and orange and crimson light through the featureless hazy air surrounding us. Even through the smoked glass goggles, I couldn't look at the suns without blinking. My eyes teared, but I didn't dare move the goggles to wipe them. If I lost my goggles, we all died.

MacConnor hung unconscious between Lucy and me, face-down, arms and legs pulled back by air pressure. The khaki lines torn out of his pants webbed the three of us together at wrists and ankles. Tethers trailed the binoculars, the first aid kit, bottles of water.

The wicker basket hung above us, slowly receding into the sky. Its greater surface area must have caused more wind resistance than its porous weave passed.

Beneath us, nothing but distant red haze fading into forever.

My left hand still felt paradoxically enormous and numb, and while my lightheadedness had faded I still felt woozy.

But best of all, my terror had gone.

We were falling into infinity, but we had a chance. A tiny chance, a chance built out of a single shaky hypothesis and a big cargo zeppelin overflowing with hope, but I'd grab that chance in my good hand and squeeze until it either carried me to safety or died in my grasp.

I tasted dusty air, rancid chicken grease and butter covering my face and lips, and life itself.

The loop of khaki rope hugging my ankle tugged. MacConnor fell faster than me, and had reached the limits of his tether. The Montague Corporation gave us tough clothing, but I didn't want to test the makeshift rope unless I absolutely had to. I pulled my arms and legs in to reduce my air resistance and sank next to him.

Lucy and I had shouted this through before jumping out. I grabbed MacConnor's shoulder with my right hand, inching myself closer and closer. MacConnor was even bigger than he looked, but eventually I had an arm over his back and a grip on his torn shirt right over his far shoulder blade. Lucy's arm brushed mine, then slithered beneath it. Her hand edged between MacConnor's ribs and mine and grabbed tight. Much more tightly than I could, with my smaller size.

I lifted my head to peer over MacConnor's head, but the wind pressure rolled his head up. I ducked down, and saw Lucy in a similar position.

Now the tricky part.

In parachute training on Earth, they teach you how to move through the air before pulling the chute—that's the "skydiving" thing. Steering is all about arranging your limbs. We needed to turn around and get our feet towards the sun.

I pulled in my free arm. We should have veered towards me, rotating towards the cliff.

Instead, our three-headed, six-legged skydiver tipped towards Lucy.

We'd talked this through, but we hadn't agreed who would steer! I thrust my numb hand back into the air. We righted out, still facing the suns.

Lucy and I nodded at each other for a moment, trying to say *You go* or *I got this*, whatever we meant. Finally, Lucy rolled her head, dragged her free arm forward into view, and slid it up against her chest.

She had the better grip—heck, she had two hands. *She* could steer. Even though this was my idea.

Slowly, we began to turn. The suns majestically rotated out of sight, leaving us with a clear view of nothing. The sun shone past our feet. Above and below and beside was only the featureless red haze. Wind blasted my face, inflated my shirt and pant legs, shoved me against MacConnor's warmth and nudged me away.

At the far edge of my vision, pale gray slowly coalesced from of the red haze: the distant cliff, still kilometers away but barely visible. Soon the world seemed split in two, with a vertical horizon separating the red glaring sky from the distant gray granite.

Finally the gray wall filled out my vision. Lucy straightened us out, and we lifted our legs to fall forward.

If we were going to have any chance at all, we needed to be closer to the cliff.

We hung in empty space.

The wind whipped my hair even as it cradled me aloft.

Skydiving training on Earth gave us two minutes of freefall. Any more than that and you had to go so high you needed breathing gear. We knew how to move forward, but I'd never thought to ask "how many *horizontal* kilometers can you cover in two minutes?" When the ground is rushing at you, you only care about the vertical.

I glanced at my watch. We'd been falling for three minutes.

The wall didn't seem any closer.

And we fell more.

My numb, bandaged hand felt even more absent. Were we even moving?

I fumbled for MacConnor's limp arm, draped it beneath me, and clamped his forearm in my left armpit. By straining my good arm, I could snatch the tether on the binoculars and reel them in. Getting the cool wooden frames to my face was another problem, but once I managed it the eyepieces clipped onto my goggles.

The cliff leaped nearer, the hazy gray resolving into muddy puddles of light and dark that oozed upward. I couldn't make out any details.

If I'd had modern electronic binocs, I'd be able to read a data feed at this range. On Freefall we only had optics mounted in a bamboo shell—the best optics our century could produce, but still, optics.

Buffeted by the wind, the binoculars tugged at my goggles.

I didn't dare lose the goggles. Reluctantly, I unclipped them. Rather than let them fly back up, however, I tucked them in the front of my shirt.

MacConnor felt warm next to me. I tried to hug him closer.

If I was wrong, the only noise I'd ever hear again was the roaring wind.

15

Two minutes of freefall is exhilarating.

An hour is tedious.

Two is just ridiculous.

Was the wall growing more green? Was the haze thinning? Did the vertical horizon creep closer? If so, it was so slow I couldn't be sure.

I made myself wait another fifteen minutes before trying the binoculars again. Working one-handed, still clinging desperately to MacConnor, I dropped them almost immediately. They fell up to jerk at the end of the khaki rope.

Lucy shook her head at me and reeled them back in.

Fine. Let her do it. I fumed at my own helplessness, my maimed hand, at the infinity beneath us. I knew it was stupid, but it beat thinking too much about the fall.

Had I killed us all?

No. Worst case, I'd changed the details of how we died.

Now that we were committed, I couldn't get rid of the horrible, growing conviction that I'd guessed wrong.

When the trauma patches wore out, and MacConnor died, should we untie him? Or should we all fall together, forever?

Then we wobbled in the air. I looked around to see Lucy holding the binoculars in front of MacConnor's face. She waved them frantically, then held still.

I weaseled my right hand free and snatched them.

Through the narrow circle of magnified vision, the gray wall had grown more detail. Were those crags? Was that a chimney? I scanned back and forth—

—wait.

That line.

That beautiful, gorgeous vertical silver line, just to our left? Maybe…

A waterfall? The famous Forever Falls?

My heart beat more quickly. We *were* closing on the wall! The waterfall was about thirty degrees off where we aimed. Lucy couldn't turn us that way, that was why she'd handed me the binoculars. I pulled in my free arm and leg, bringing us closer to our target.

The wall grew. And grew.

Details became clearer and clearer, until I could see the waterfall without the binoculars.

It turns out that on Freefall you can crawl about six horizontal kilometers an hour, as you plunge eleven hundred kilometers straight down. That's only, what: one hundred eighty or so to one?

We paused about two hundred meters from the cliff, the beautiful bottomless cliff, just to the left of the river. We didn't want to hit an unexpected outcropping. The chimneys and crevasses and outcroppings were only streaks as we plummeted, the river a blur.

Maybe the river ended in a nice deep pool. A bottomless pool.

We didn't have to die of thirst. Maybe we'd get the chance to drown instead.

Or maybe the last of us would surrender to despair, and kiss that wall.

But for now, we rearranged our lines.

We tugged ourselves closer together, MacConnor on the bottom, Lucy and I flank to flank above him.

And fell faster.

16

What's to say?

Weak from blood loss, constantly abraded by the ceaseless wind of freefall, I grew thirstier and thirstier. After three hours, we'd finished the water.

Four hours in, Lucy had to shift her bowels. That was neither fun nor dignified. Fortunately, we fell faster than the results. I felt glad I'd lost yesterday's lunch, and wore yesterday's dinner on my face and hands.

We'd planned the wait. We'd have hours and hours of tedium ahead. If I was right, at the end we'd have about two desperate minutes—assuming we noticed in time. We absolutely had to keep watch. We grew deft at quickly trading the binoculars and fitting them onto the goggles.

The world felt sideways. The suns were at our feet, the ground at our head, and we fell sideways faster than the speed of sound. Had we left a sonic boom all those kilometers behind? What was the speed of sound on Freefall, anyway?

A pillow of winds cradled me. It would have been easy to fall asleep there, with MacConnor plunging beneath me. My body ached for rest, real rest, in an actual bed or just a cold granite floor. My bruises and sprains grew more and more insistent, dull aches that blossomed into full-fledged pains.

For long minutes I peered downward, with the red sky at our feet and the granite wall flashing by overhead in streaks of green and gray, the waterfall a wavering ribbon, the binoculars pressing the goggles into my eye sockets. When the hypnotic weave of gray and green and silver threatened to overwhelm me, I wrenched the binoculars off my face and passed them to Lucy.

I grew thirstier. And thirstier.

Eight hours in, the trauma patch on my maimed left hand started wearing off. Pain from that injury started seeping back in.

Before long, I had to blink tears back from my eyes. The protective grease of my face had long since ablated away, and the dry wind felt like a cool sandblaster over my face, my neck, the slope of my breasts and hands. The khaki rope that had felt soft hours ago had now abraded its brand around my wrist, and another had burned through my sock and now left a blood-speckled ring around my ankle.

We had the first aid kit.

It had trauma packs, all in paper wrappers. I had no doubt that Lucy would fight like hell to get one out for me. And she would get one.

The wind would steal the rest.

If I could stand it a little longer, ride out the little bit of painkiller remaining in my system, I'd get the full benefit. Another eight peaceful hours.

But MacConnor was hurt worse than me. A lot worse, with the stab wounds in his chest and gut. And we'd put him on point, so the wind must be burning his exposed skin utterly raw. We'd even stolen his damn pants for this stunt. Maybe he should get the last trauma pack.

Ultimately, it didn't matter.

We would die falling.

MacConnor was the worst hurt. He'd die first.

Maybe he was already dead, the lucky bastard.

Lucy was battered, but not maimed.

She'd outlive me.

I wished her luck.

And peace.

If, at the end, she guided us into the cliff, I'd forgive her.

And that's all there was.

I was resting, eyes closed, trying to focus on my breath rather than on my growing distress, when Lucy jabbed me in the chest, *hard*, with the binoculars.

My eyes flashed open. I blinked away tears.

She shook the binoculars in front of my face.

Insane hope flashed inside me. I grabbed the binoculars and wrenched them to my eyes.

Lucy was already struggling with the rope around her ankle.

The binoculars fought me and I struggled to get them onto my face. They slipped and fumbled, my hand shaking, but I managed to snap them into place and peer down.

In a world of gray and green and hazy reds and orange, something gleamed silver. Far below us, it seemed to fly closer even between blinks.

The Debris Shield.

I'd been right.

Takamoto hadn't dragged Gupper up.

He'd shoved Gupper over the edge.

Dropping him *down*.

This universe looped back on itself.

17

We plunged through endless space—no, endlessly *repeating* space. The hazy ochre sky and flashing, streaky granite cliff suddenly seemed gorgeous. Adrenalin and endorphins flooded my blood, shoving back my saturating pain. The trailing streamers of first-aid kit and tattered clothes and loops of slack line transformed into our victory banners.

My teeth bared in a rabid, victorious grin, and the wind inflated my parched cheeks into a flapping farce.

I still felt exhausted. The eternal wind had sucked every drop of moisture from my body. I'd lost blood. My bisected right hand hurt like a horde of angry insects had nested in the palm. My other wrist ached from the chafing of the loop of rope around it, and the leashed ankle burned even worse.

But we had a chance.

Takamoto had killed one person. He'd tried to kill three more.

I would *not* give him a shot at anyone else. That chubby bastard was going all the way down—and I was *the* expert on just how far down that was.

Ecstatic fire lit my nerves.

MacConnor hung beside me. Was he still alive? Had the trauma patches kept him together? I looked at his pale face and wanted to hug him. Ridiculous paintbrush mustache or no, I'd have dinner with him.

Lucy looked a lot more like some Irish warrior ancestor. Her jaw had grown firm, and even through the smoked goggles I thought I saw fire in her eyes. Her red hair stood up in a ridiculous tangle, black dust and gray grease streaked her face, but at that moment she would have charged a lion if we'd had one handy.

Lucy's hand clasped mine. She mouthed *thank you* and gave me a grin almost as wild as my own. Then she slipped a bloody khaki rope from around her wrist, setting herself free.

Her chute box exploded.

Lucy shot into the sky in a flash of silver.

Had the chute held against this wind?

Or had it blown, triggering the backup chute?

Had her backup chute held?

I might never know.

We'd argued about who would launch MacConnor. She had two hands. I had the training for stupid physical activities.

I'd won.

But I wished I hadn't.

I knocked the binoculars off my face, letting them soar to the end of their tether. I didn't need them anymore.

Terminal velocity: eighteen kilometers a minute.

Maximum visibility: fifty kilometers.

How much time had passed?

Had Lucy noticed the Debris Shield's gleam right away? Or had it taken thirty seconds? Sixty seconds?

Did the Facility's radar point up? If so, they would have noticed Lucy's radar-reflective parachute. Were zeppelin pilots already scrambling to pick her up?

Or were they oblivious?

A computer would notice and scream. Computers didn't work on Freefall.

If I fell past the Facility, if I got our chutes open late, would they even notice us?

I didn't let myself look down, instead attacking the line attaching my ankle to MacConnor's. Eight hours of intermittent tugging had inexorably tightened the knot, and my own wind-dried blood cemented it, but I jammed a thumb beneath the slipknot and wrenched it back and forth until my heel slipped past the loop and I kicked the line free.

That left the line on my good wrist.

I couldn't loosen the knot around my right wrist with my right hand. Instead, I attacked MacConnor's end with fingers and teeth.

My heart pounded in my chest. How much time did we have? Seconds?

The knot fought me, and fought more, but I dragged it off his wrist.

For half a second we hung in space, my legs wrapped around his thigh, my good fist in the tattered rags of his shirt.

MacConnor looked like hell. He might be dead.

I would not believe he was dead. Not after all this. I remembered his eyes well enough to see them through the smoked glass goggles. His chest, lined with the taut muscles of someone who worked for a living. And that chipper fearlessness. That chin.

Stubble—he was alive!

No, hair grew after death.

If we made it, if we both actually stood on solid floor again, dinner was not the only thing I would get out of him.

I released my hand and loosened my legs so he could drift free.

Grabbed the tag of his chute box.

And yanked.

MacConnor exploded out of my grasp like a shotgun blast.

Some part of him smacked my chin—a leg? a hand?

My vision went gray around the edges.

My precarious balance shattered.

MacConnor vanished into the sky, and I corkscrew-tumbled down.

18

The world whirled around me.

Red sky filled my vision, then gray-green granite wall, then sky, flickering contrast sprayed across the kaleidoscope in my rattled skull. My teeth hurt where MacConnor's parting shot had smashed my chin. Centripetal force rushed fresh blood to my crippled hand. The baleful wind battered my ears. My mouth tasted bright and coppery on my swollen tongue.

I couldn't tell where I was. We'd kept our distance to a couple hundred meters from the cliff, but had we closed on it as I struggled free of MacConnor?

I knew how to straighten out of this spin. It would take a few seconds.

Never pull a chute while you're tumbling. You might tangle yourself in the shroud, and then you're done.

But how far above the Facility was I?

I knew how things worked now. But wounded, I couldn't survive another eight hours of desiccating freefall.

If I missed the Facility, I died.

I brought my hand to the tag on my chute box and yanked.

The straps through my crotch and along my chest kicked me, hurtling me through the sky like a soccer ball. My limbs seemed to trail behind, the hips and shoulders and knees and elbows all screaming in surprise, my pelvis and shoulders screeching in outrage at the impact.

The wind's roar deepened, its first change in hours. My numbed ears suddenly felt alive.

Blood left my head. The world turned gray.

I lost my thoughts, only knowing that I had to stay conscious. I *had* to.

I felt, rather than heard, something snap. A whole harp of strings, stretched beyond any possible limit, twanging and breaking in a row.

The wind's roar started surging up again.

The backup chute detonated out of my pack, a second impact on my battered body.

Silence rang in my ears.

My wind-abraded face and hands blossomed into a full scorching burn.

But the cliff was moving. Crags of rock. *Individual* crags, not a blur. Water splashed, only meters away.

I should have hovered, but instead the cliff roared past me. How fast was I going? I glanced up. The steering vents had torn away from the silver expanse of the parachute. The reserve chute had held, barely, but air poured through the gaps where vents should have billowed.

I might be able to steer. Sort of.

How fast could a zeppelin scramble?

Had they noticed me?

I glanced down.

The Debris Shield was maybe a kilometer beneath me—no, less. And closing fast.

I couldn't see MacConnor or Lucy.

They had to be above me.

They *had* to be.

The rule was: wait for a zeppelin. Hang in midair and await rescue. But I wasn't hanging in midair. I was falling, nowhere near terminal velocity, but faster than I should be. Maybe faster than a zeppelin could fly.

I shook my head.

With my throbbing hand and burning skin, with the bruises and strains and sprains, saving my own life felt like too much trouble. But there was MacConnor. And Lucy.

And Takamoto.

Takamoto was *not* going to get away with murdering us.

I aimed the plunging chute at the shining steel length of the Debris Shield.

19

The chute straps rolled and shifted against the fresh bruises in my pelvis and shoulders. My wind-stunned ears heard nothing but a constant ringing that echoed through every battered sinew and bone. In my goggles, the long, narrow Debris Shield swelled.

A slim step of safety.

Or a long fall to a painful death.

Or, maybe, a quick crash against the green granite cliff that loomed to the infinite ends of the universe.

I felt like a mummified corpse, drained of fluid and baked in desert sands for a thousand years, reanimated by some cruel curse to wreak vengeance from beyond the grave.

I wondered if Takamoto had ever seen those old movies.

No, get help. Send zeppelins to catch MacConnor and Lucy. Then Takamoto.

The Debris Shield grew in my vision.

The parachute loomed overhead. How big was it? Could I land on the Debris Shield? Or would the canopy's edge brush the jagged granite cliff before my feet touched the riveted steel awning?

Only one way to find out, Redding. My best chance was to land at the edge of the awning.

I turned so my momentum would carry me towards the cliff.

The Debris Shield raced at me.

You're supposed to hold the chute straps when you land, but my screaming-maimed left hand wasn't going to be touching anything, ever again, as far as I was concerned.

I bent my knees and took a deep breath.

My feet slammed into the Debris Shield.

I exhaled explosively, shouting in victory, crashing forward, trying to roll uphill, each touch of sun-heated metal slapping bruises and strains. My wounded hand rolled under me and I screamed, the sudden flash of pain and pressure almost wiping my thoughts away.

Seconds later, I lay on my back, still.

My ears rang. I hurt absolutely *everywhere.*

But the hot steel of the Debris Shield, a line of rivets scorching my back, felt better than the pillow of winds ever had. I could have lain there forever.

The chute billowed down towards me. An updraft caught it, tugging it back up.

Tangled shroud lines yanked at my shoulders.

My hand scrabbled for the buckles at my chest. I was *not* going to let the parachute haul me over the edge. Not now. By the time I thrashed my way clear of the enmeshing lines, I was on my feet, a couple feet from the granite cliff. The heat was incredible— that cliff had absorbed the constant warmth of countless suns since the beginning of time. Radiant heat scalded my tenderized hide, but barely registered next to the throbbing in my maimed paw.

The weightless chute huffed up. Abandoned lines skittered across the shining steel. Then the whole thing floated over the edge of the Debris Shield and down into oblivion.

So long, friend.

My legs begged to buckle. Instead I stumbled down the stairs, the beautiful metal-grille stairs with the octagonal Montague stamp in the center of each. The sunscorched steel rail burned the palm of my functional hand as I lurched down. At that moment I could have sucked the water out of a slice of dehydrated apple. The stairs seemed to wobble and weave beneath me, but I clambered down, yanked the access door open, wrenched the goggles off my face, and made myself trot, lumbering and lurching, down the access hall.

The first person I found was a beefy A/C technician, crouched at an open access panel, his head almost inside the cooling system. I tried to say *Hey you*, but what came out was more of a coughing screech.

He turned from his work, annoyance naked on his face. His gaze met my eyes, and the annoyance instantly dissolved to stark terror. He fell back from his crouch, hitting his butt.

I coughed again, clearing my throat. "Rescue zeppelins," I croaked, trying to be heard over the high-pitched screech in my ears. "Two people. Call."

He blinked owlishly at me, mouth working helplessly. I guessed *he* had seen those old mummy films.

I coughed again, trying to clear my throat enough to speak. "Two people. Zeppelin wreck. Get help!"

The alarm klaxons blew, audible even to my stunned ears.

The tech's eyes grew wide. He scrabbled back, crab-walking on hands and feet, jaw flapping.

The klaxon stopped and a panicked voice shouted "This is not a drill" over the loudspeaker. "Emergency zeppelin crews, launch. We have three—no, four—contacts, moving fast. Too fast. But they're chutes. Ten, twelve kilometers up. Repeat, this is not a drill. Zeppelin crews, scramble."

The operator sounded panicked. Forecourt would have his head for that. Security folks could lose their cool, but they could never sound like it.

The technician stopped scrabbling away and peered at me in confusion. His mouth formed words.

"Two people," I said, holding up two fingers. My ears rang too badly. My tongue felt like a dry rust-soaked sponge. "Only two people." Was I even understandable?

Then I turned and lurched towards the inside stairs. They lurched and spun beneath me, but I clutched the handrail and made it down the single flight I needed without slipping and breaking my neck.

Lucy. MacConnor.

Takamoto.

The upper annex was a big open room where the elevators started and a dozen big corridors connected. When I slammed the stairwell door open, two chatting technicians in white coats walking from the elevators looked at me and froze mid-step and mid-word.

I glared at them.

They both stepped back, hands raised.

I lurched across the annex to the security office door and flung it open.

The upper security office combined a front desk for visitors to request help, backed by a locker room where we security types stashed equipment and changed clothes. Skinny Tara Beaner bent her head over an open ledger on the front desk. "Yes," she said without taking her gaze from the paper. My stunned ears could barely decipher the words. "Can I—"

She looked up and froze.

Her mouth worked. "Redding?"

I ignored her. My sight suddenly zeroed in on the refreshment table behind the desk.

A pitcher.

A glass pitcher.

Of *water*.

Drops of condensation trickled down its outside.

I lunged.

Beaner jumped to her feet, shouting something.

I had the pitcher in my hand. Cool water burned my windscorched palm, my battered fingers, my inflamed lips, and then gushed into my mouth, shocking cold, a flame that burned my palate and slicked my ashen throat and hit my stomach like an explosion of life.

Everything had happened too fast. It abruptly hit me with the clean cool taste of water.

I'd done it.

We'd done the impossible.

I was going to live.

Lucy would live.

And if MacConnor had made it this far—

I lowered the pitcher. The water cascaded through me, exploding outward, resurrecting desiccated tissue and strengthening my legs. My vision seemed to clear with each blink.

I coughed again, and this time my words felt almost intelligible. "Zeppelins. Two people. Tell them."

"Redding!" Beaner said, stepping towards me. "How are you still alive?" Her eyes flicked from my face, to my torso, to the filthy bandage on my hand, growing more dismayed at each step.

"Later." I chugged another mouthful of water. Drinking too fast would make me ill, but my body screamed for more, to down the whole pitcher and steal the full one beside it. "Two people. Parachutes. Lucy Cedar. MacConnor, pilot. Tell. Them."

Beaner grabbed the phone. "Two people. Parachutes. Got it."

They'd rescue Lucy and MacConnor. I'd done everything I could to save them.

Takamoto.

One killing? Maybe an accident. Things happen.

But *four* murders?

Something had broken inside him.

He'd kill again.

Maybe he was killing now.

Whatever it took, I would stop Takamoto. He would go down, if I had to grab his flabby neck and plunge over the edge with him.

20

For a second I wavered on my feet. The water, the blessed water rehydrating my flesh, hadn't hit my brain yet. While the rest of my absurdly battered body sparked when the water spread that far, my thoughts either hadn't cleared yet or the shock of survival clouded them further.

Tara Beaner, behind the unpolished green granite security desk, machine-gunned words into the phone handset while staring at me in appalled horror. Once she hung that phone up, she'd call other security officers to help her.

Help her restrain me.

Thought oozed through my skull like toxic sludge.

Restrain me? That was *not* going to happen.

Lucy's life, MacConnor's life, were in someone else's hands now.

Takamoto.

The upper security office had a weapons locker. The glass-doored cabinet stood right behind Beaner. Each day I checked out a taser at the beginning of shift and returned it at the end.

But above the tasers—the flechette pistols. A thousand tiny razor blades in each shell. The glass in front of them said *BREAK IN CASE OF EMERGENCY*. A single flechette round would strip Takamoto's greasy meat off his—

I made myself stop that thought.

That wasn't the way.

Stopping Takamoto meant finding him. An internal security alert. I needed authority. In the security team, that meant—

"Where is"—*cough*—"Forecourt?"

"Down in Zeppelin Security." Beaner's voice sounded thin, and it wasn't just the ringing in my ears.

I engulfed another mouthful of water. That dragged my body past some critical level, and rancid festering sweat erupted from every pore. My air-blasted skin screeched at the violation, but that wasn't anything next to my bruises. My torqued knee—when had *that* happened? What remained of my left hand screeched. "Sublevel eight?"

"Seven."

I slammed the half-empty pitcher down on the table, handle muddy from my touch, and grabbed the full one. "Two people. One hurt. Tell them."

Beaner looked me up and down. "*One* hurt?"

I ignored her and tottered towards the door, precious water sloshing from the brimming pitcher.

"Aidan—wait!"

"Takamoto," I croaked. "Gotta—stop—Takamoto."

The elevator arrived only seconds after I rang the bell, steel doors gliding silently open. The elevator operator in his old-fashioned red jacket with the silver buttons, said "Hello, where can I—" Then he actually looked at me.

I staggered in, water slopping wastefully out of the brimming pitcher. "Sublevel seven. Security issue. Emergency. Do *not* stop."

He gaped, then frantically grabbed the lever and put the car in gear.

I sagged against the back wall, gulped another mouthful of water. My body seemed to be coming back to life around me. The elixir of life, raising me from the dead.

But the mirror steel elevator doors showed a different film.

My black hair stood straight up from my head, glued there by grease and dried sweat. Fresh sweat coursed down my brow, my cheeks.

My caramel skin? What wasn't black from dirty grease was wind-blasted red. When the endorphins ran down I'd sink into screaming pain.

My clothes were torn. My shirt had a single button left, exposing my bellybutton and my bra. I wasn't big enough to fly out of the bra, but flopping free couldn't have made me look any worse.

The soiled bandage on my maimed hand was turning red. I'd torn the wound back open, probably when I crushed the hand between the Debris Shield and my stomach. Blood ran down the pale, immobile fingers.

A red drop appeared at the end of my index finger, swelled, and plunged to the floor.

I stank of fear and sickly fever sweat, rotting chicken fat and rancid butter.

The elevator operator kept his head squarely forward, but repeatedly stole glances at me from the corner of his eyes. I smiled at him—well, exposed a few teeth—and gulped rich, luscious water as quickly as I dared.

Sublevel Seven handled logistics for the cargo zeppelins and all the other paperwork required by a big shipping operation. Big men in hardhats, QA techs in safety glasses and steel-toed boots, file clerks, all stepped aside as I shambled down the main hall. More than one person offered help. I quaffed water from my pitcher and marched on.

Security Third Keith Werner stood outside the door of the big Zeppelin Security office, hands behind his back. Whatever was going on in there, Forecourt didn't want to be disturbed.

Too bad for her.

Keith noticed me. His hand scrabbled for his taser, then recognition grew in his eyes. "Aidan? Holy—I mean, what? Aidan!" He raised his hands as if to catch me before I collapsed.

I shouldered past him, seized the doorknob of the Zeppelin Security room, and body-slammed it open.

Behind me, Keith shouted "Hey, you can't—"

The slamming door cut him off.

The big conference room in the front of Zeppelin Security was full. Yes, Forecourt sat at the table, but so did Facility President Ford. The chief zeppelin mechanic, the senior physician, the head of Research.

And in the corner furthest from the door, fenced in by two of Security's biggest thugs, huddled Takamoto.

Conversation stopped instantly. Shock, surprise, and a little fascinated horror filled the room of faces.

I lifted the pitcher. It was almost empty, so I tipped it all the way back. The excess water coursing down my chin, my shirt, felt almost as delicious as that final swallow sloshing down my throat.

Then I lurched forward to the closest edge of the polished granite table.

Slammed the pitcher down with a sound like breaking stone.

My maimed hand came up on its own. Blood seeped through the bandage and dripped from my dead white fingers onto the table.

I pointed at Takamoto, who was shrinking back even further into the corner.

My throat no longer grated, but my voice burbled like a plague victim as I snarled, "*You. Killed. GUPPER.*"

Takamoto's face turned as white as the sheets of paper scattered around the table, and he raised his hands to protect his face. "I didn't mean to! It was an accident!"

I stood still, hand outstretched, eyes wide and probably a little insane.

Takamoto babbled, "I was eating breakfast on the balcony and he came up. The bastard bragged to me about bagging Cedar. He knew how I felt about her. Losing's one thing, but he rubbed it in!"

Another drop of blood plunged from my hand.

"I hit him," Takamoto said desperately. "He hit back, then we were fighting and he slipped through the rail! It was an accident! I swear."

I imagined falling from the rail. Seeing infinity sprawl beneath me.

No chute box.

Drying out. Burning from the wind.

Deciding to not steer myself into the wall. Choosing the long way down.

Making that decision over and over again.

The silver of the Debris Shield rising from the depths.

Gupper could have steered clear of it. He could have lived a few hours longer.

But he hadn't.

I worked my lips. "Gupper died. To tell us. You murdered him. Bravest. Thing. I've ever seen."

Takamoto's eyes rolled back. He fainted into his chair.

The first good idea the bastard had.

MacConnor? Lucy? Check.

Takamoto? Check.

Everything all taken care of, then.

I think someone caught my head before I hit the ground.

21

I came to slowly, with an ecstatic absence of pain. White sheets. Actual white ceiling tiles, soft white sound baffles with granite peeking around them. A mattress, less accommodating than the endlessly adaptable air but far preferable. Antiseptic stung my nose.

Someone had cleaned me, probably with a hose and a long brush, then drenched my burns with a wonderful soothing lotion.

I rolled my neck. No pain, but my hair had been trimmed. Probably not a bad idea.

My teeth. My teeth were *clean*. I tasted mint.

Someone said, "She's awake." I would have argued, but that would have required being awake.

But the male voice sounded clear in my ears. No ringing. I hadn't permanently damaged my hearing.

The nurse had just wrapped his brand-new but antique blood pressure cuff around my arm when Forecourt walked in. Was the Second a little flushed? Had she run here, halting only outside the door to recover her composure? Not that I'd ever done that.

"Redding," she said, standing laser-straight. "About time you were up."

"You know me." My throat felt better than it should, but my voice was too quiet. The pain was gone, but I still felt tired. "Slacking every chance."

Forecourt narrowed her eyes at the nurse.

Unruffled, he noted my blood pressure in the chart and met Forecourt's glare. "Five minutes." He tucked the cuff into a supply closet and strolled out.

"Damn Medical," Forecourt said. "Think they run the place."

I didn't say anything. Insulting the medical staff while I was laid up didn't seem smart.

But speaking of smart, I hadn't been that smart earlier. When I reached the first security office I could have told Tara Beaner to get Forecourt and trigger an alarm on Takamoto. Instead I'd charged down there and confronted him myself.

Not smart. I felt good about running him down, but: not smart.

But now Forecourt would hand me my scalp for it.

"So," Forecourt said, in her usual quiet voice. "Coming back from the dead. You've raised the bar for all of us. You know that, don't you?"

"I do my best, sir." I licked my lips. "What about Lucy—Cedar? And MacConnor?"

"Lucy's fine. They stabilized MacConnor, shipped him back through the Portal to Earth. By now he's annoying the hospital staff in Montevideo. Which you'll be doing yourself pretty soon."

I blinked. "Sir?" I'd been *cashiered*?

She frowned. "You hadn't—they didn't tell you?" Forecourt cast an evil look at the doorway. "Your hand, Redding."

I raised my hands. The fingers of the right were battered and red, still gleaming with mint-scented medicated salve. A heavy bandage covered the left.

The bandage ended too soon.

Soft isn't the same thing as gentle, but Forecourt's voice became both. "You lost the hand. Cedar told us the whole story."

"She kept us together," I said weakly. The empty space where my fingers had been unsettled me. I waved my remaining fingers through the gap, inches from the bandaged stump.

"You'll have your hand back in two weeks," Forecourt said. "Two more weeks medical leave. The question is, what do you want after that?"

"Sir?"

"Cedar told us how you figured out Freefall, when nobody else had. I know, nobody else had Gupper's example."

"Or motivation."

Forecourt flashed a quick but sincere smile. "Oh, yes. Never discount motivation." Her gaze wandered away from me, towards the shelf of supplies. "I knew the story around Gupper didn't add up. It didn't make sense. I sent you to ask questions to give you some experience."

Was that a note of... *apology* in Forecourt's voice?

"Then you wanted the special flight. You had the credentials. I couldn't go myself. We don't have a better candidate. I pushed you a little, to see if you'd stick by your observations. To see how far you'd go." Forecourt pulled in a deep breath. "I had no idea that someone would try to cover up one murder with three more. I apologize. I've already submitted a negative report on myself to headquarters. You're free to do the same."

I closed my eyes, thinking. The bed's comfort felt seductive. "You gave me a chance," I said. "I wanted the chance."

"It's my job to keep my people safe."

I laughed. "We're hanging like bugs on the side of a cliff that goes down forever. Safe is not— I mean—"

"Still."

I opened my eyes again. "They have me drugged up, don't they?"

"Oh, yes. You have the good stuff."

"Then I won't decide anything now, but—no. Thanks, but no."

Forecourt's sigh was both relieved and regretful. "Once you finish therapy, you'll need to decide where you want to go. It's Montague policy that people can resign after a traumatic injury. Given what you went through and what you learned and the people you saved, you're due one hell of a bonus payment. You could live the next five years in luxury, or invest it and never work a day again. Or, you're welcome back here. I wondered how far you'd go, and the answer is all the way and back again. You're welcome in any team I lead. Or I'll recommend you for any Montague placement you want."

"The Hindenbarge." The words popped out of my mouth, but my brain agreed when it caught up.

Forecourt leaned back. "Why there?"

"Because I haven't yet."

"Fair enough," Forecourt laughed. Her voice grew softer, even conspiratorial. "I had everybody in there leaning on Takamoto, digging at every weak spot in his story. We knew he'd cut you free, we guessed why, but we couldn't get the details out of him. And then you stormed in, all blood and death, and—and—just wow." A grin split her face. "The next time I need someone to confess, I'm getting the murder victim to walk in just like you did."

This time, I laughed with her.

Keep reading for a glimpse of the next Aidan Redding Montague Portal novel:

Hydrogen Sleets

The Montague Corporation didn't exactly cancel my vacation. They just made it boring. I was in a modest green bikini, sunbathing on a chaise of almost insubstantial molecular mesh and enjoying the Congolese rainforest resort's brilliant clear sunlight and humid tropical fug, when my datalink chirped. "Montague Human Resources for Aidan Redding."

The company had an unexpected opening for a bottom-level security position.

I could have said no. Montague considers vacation time sacred, and I had two months until my next assignment.

But a surprise opening for a security third? Two months in another universe? A universe I wouldn't get to see otherwise?

I'd grown up burning to see the universes. Yes, all infinity of them.

Even if I ignored the weeks of medical leave I'd needed to get my hand regrown, I'd had a month of actual vacation. I'd visited my parents—on their anniversary, no less. Their delighted surprise still danced in my heart, but a week in the barrio had been plenty. Any longer, and the gap between us got too uncomfortable.

And the Congolese rainforest resort would be here when I returned.

Whenever that was.

Normally, assignment to a new universe requires anything from a week to a month of classroom and physical training before you get near the Portal.

Montague wanted to send me—immediately?

I'd never heard of such a thing. Which didn't mean it didn't happen, only that it'd never happened to me. The thought that I might already have sufficient training flared through my head and just as quickly died. *Nobody* had all the training needed to enter a brand-new universe.

By the time the HR system disconnected, I was already stuffing my French-Spanish phrase book into my bag and my feet into my sandals. Before I reached the airport outside Lubumbashi, they'd sent the tickets and a quarter million words of briefing to my datalink. I swept through customs and onto the Congolese Air ballistic glider, and found myself upgraded to first class. I didn't have time for the complimentary massage or the open bar—the forty-five-minute flight back to Uruguay gave me barely enough time to snatch a few important names from the dossier and memorize the universe summary.

Meet the new universe, same as the old universe.

But thirteen billion years younger.

A Montague car met me at the airport—not an automatic, a limousine. With an actual human driver, a young man hired for charm instead of brains. I noticed the vat-leather seats and the driver's half-flirting repartee, but buried myself in the Physical Environment part of the briefing. I could learn everyone's names and the org chart later, but if this universe's natural laws said "inhale and you'll explode," I needed to know right away. The driver recognized the symptoms and he didn't seem upset.

A brand-new universe—brand-new to me, yes, but also literally a newborn. Only a few hundred million years after its Big Bang. Full of nothing but hydrogen screaming out of that primal blast, torrents of cosmic rays…

And an old-fashioned space station.

Six concentric rings spun for gravity.

Eight spokes connecting them.

A weightless bubble at the core, full of telescopes.

A million tons of metal, protected from the cosmic hurricane by carefully balanced magnetic fields, with antennas and sensors sticking out everywhere. The same magnetic fields sieved hydrogen from the void to fuel the fusion reactors powering the whole thing.

Straight out of a second millennium movie.

Humanity couldn't reach the stars, but we'd weaseled our way into deep space anyway.

Excitement fluttered my pulse all the way to the Portal.

*

One step between the electrodes of the Portal, and my weight plunged twenty percent.

It's not like I weigh much anyway, but the sudden weight shift set my inner ear whirling and made me wobble. I automatically grabbed for the cool aluminum handrail—not that I saw it, but there's always a handrail outside the Portal.

A petite leather-gloved hand with a grip like a bear trap seized my bicep and said "Easy, ma'am, it hits everyone that way."

"Thanks." I took a breath of fresh but metallic air to steady myself.

About the size of a subway station, the Portal chamber's aluminum ceiling arched away from me, decorated by regular lines of rivets and the occasional octagonal Montague stamp. Electronic equipment and screens lined the walls, along with boxes of cargo bound in and out. Two women in khaki stood further back, one behind a slender touchscreen console, the other with a laser rifle aimed at me.

I didn't take the rifle personally. Returning to Earth, you appeared in a sealed box. If *those* scanners detected anything harmful, you'd never know it. Montague's zeal in protecting Earth from alien universes would seem maniacal, if the risks weren't so horrific. On my first assignment, an egotistical researcher had tried to carry half a kilogram of antimatter ore back to Earth. It was harmless in its native universe, but on Earth it would have knocked South America into orbit.

The little East Asian guy holding my arm wore too much sharp cologne, the smell like a barbed-wire blanket. His uniform hung too loose over his shoulders. Sensor goggles hugged his eye sockets, presenting him with a billion details about everything they picked up. He had PERCIVAL stitched above the pocket of his khaki uniform shirt. "You okay?" His voice seemed weirdly deep from such a tiny frame.

"Yeah."

Percival's goggled gaze moved up and down my body, insultingly direct. I knew he wasn't leering, but I always felt uncomfortable with someone studying me so closely. The Portal's mathematical transformations might have altered me dangerously, or changed harmless bacteria into something nightmarish, and the goggles would show that. They also exposed my skin in a display that would make a strip joint operator envious. I made myself stand still.

After a few tense heartbeats Percival said "Clear. Welcome aboard Wemm Station, Miss Redding."

"Thanks. Where's HR?"

Percival shook his head. "Y'all don't get HR." He held out a gleaming black brand-new datalink in his gloved hand. "We have instructions to send you straight to Six. Leave your bag, we'll get it to your quarters."

"Six?" Disquiet tickled my spine. The local Human Resources person should explain the rules, introduce me to my team, and give me the tour. And the tour would presumably include where the heck this *Six* was.

"Ring Six?" Percival frowned. "How much briefing did you get, anyway?"

"They *sent* the whole thing. I had maybe half an hour to read it."

Percival tightened his lips. "Don't y'all worry, we'll get you up to speed." He jerked his hand towards the door. "Out them double doors. Turn right. Montague elevator on your right. Sixth ring. It's right by the Core, so there's no gravity. Hang onto the elevator rail as you go up, or y'all'll smack the ceiling. Tell me you at least done the free-fall training?"

You have no *idea.* "Yes."

Percival nodded. "Security First Watford's waiting for y'all."

Straight to the top? That could *not* be good. "Thanks." I plucked the palm-sized datalink from his hand. The black plastic rectangle shimmered as it sampled my DNA, then chirped, "Aidan Redding. Montague Corporation. Security Third."

"Confirm," I said.

The datalink buzzed as it sucked my personal settings out of the local datacore.

"Come by at dinner," Percival said. "I'll introduce y'all to the team."

"Thanks!" I clipped the datalink to my belt and broke into a trot towards the double doors at the far end of the room.

No introduction. No tour. Not even a map.

For the first time, I wondered why Montague had an unexpected urgent opening here in a universe that held nothing besides hydrogen and cosmic rays. Was I replacing someone? And if so—why?

About the Author

https://mwl.io

Never miss another new release!
Sign up for Michael Warren Lucas' mailing list at
http://mwl.io.

Novels:
Immortal Clay
Kipuka Blues
Butterfly Stomp Waltz
Hydrogen Sleets
git commit murder

Nonfiction (as Michael W Lucas):
Relayd and Httpd Mastery – PAM Mastery – FreeBSD Mastery: Advanced ZFS
– FreeBSD Mastery: Specialty Filesystems – FreeBSD Mastery: ZFS – Tarsnap
Mastery – Networking for Systems Administrators – FreeBSD Mastery: Storage
Essentials – Sudo Mastery – DNSSEC Mastery – Absolute OpenBSD – SSH
Mastery – Network Flow Analysis – Absolute FreeBSD – Cisco Routers for the
Desperate – PGP & GPG

See your favorite bookstore for more!

www.ingramcontent.com/pod-product-compliance
Lightning Source LLC
Chambersburg PA
CBHW020533120726
47904CB00003B/1048